Praise for Beth Williamson's *The Gift*

5 Lyras "...an action-packed novel with suspense, danger, and a truly despicable villain. The reader is also treated to an abundance of sexual tension, red-hot sex, and good old-fashioned romance...The Gift is the fifth book of the Malloy family series. Be warned that once you read this book, you'll want to read the rest of the books in the series. "

~ *Susan Park, Rites of Romance Reviews*

5 Angels and a Recommended Read "The Malloys have been a favorite for this reader and I loved this next book...Beth Williamson out did herself with this beautiful story for its got passion and a romance that shines like all the Malloy stories do and keeps the love for this family going strong."

~ *Lena C, Fallen Angel Reviews*

5 Lips "Another great turnout by Beth Williamson! She does an extraordinary job with character development, historical settings and adds just the right amount of humor, suspense and emotional rhetoric to keep you entertained from start to finish!...If you like historical westerns, this, as well as the others in this series – all of which this reviewer's read, is a must read. You'll never be disappointed..."

~ *Joni, TwoLips Reviews*

5 Blue Ribbons "THE GIFT, in true Beth Williamson style, swept me away for a wonderful afternoon of reading. Secretly smiling at Trevor's dilemma, I adored him for the charmer and bad boy he was and I applauded him for the man he becomes. Adelaide quickly gained my respect for her strong independence and her capable self-reliance."

~:*Natasha Smith, Romance Junkies*

4.5 Stars, Heat Level H "Trevor's interaction with Adelaide is fiery and their scenes together simply sizzle, with some meltingly hot sex between them. This sexy romantic historical is packed with action, voyeurism, and some very steamy scenes that will give the reader a buzz."

~ *Aggie Tsirikas, Just Erotic Romance Reviews*

The Gift

Beth Williamson

A Samhain Publishing, Ltd. publication.

Samhain Publishing, Ltd.
512 Forest Lake Drive
Warner Robins, GA 31093
www.samhainpublishing.com

The Gift

Print ISBN: 1-59998-367-2
Digital ISBN: 1-59998-169-6

Editing by Sasha Knight
Cover by Scott Carpenter

First Samhain Publishing, Ltd. electronic publication: November 2006
First Samhain Publishing, Ltd. print publication: February 2007

Dedication

To my sister Tammy who shows me that each and every day is a gift to be savored. Much love.

Chapter One

Cheshire, Wyoming, May 1889

In the corner of the saloon lit only by half a dozen gas lanterns, Trevor Malloy cupped the deliciously round ass in front of him and squeezed. "Sugar, you need to set yourself right on my lap," he purred.

A purely feminine giggle floated down to him. "You know I can't, sweetie. I'm working."

He smiled and patted her sweet behind. "I've got all night, Mindy."

Mindy flipped one brown curl over her shoulder and winked. "Maybe you'll see me later then."

Trevor returned the wink and took a gulp of his beer. He watched her sashay away, her well-endowed breasts bouncing, her ass jiggling. All of it made his blood simmer and the easy burn of arousal slide through him. Mindy knew how to behave herself in bed, or not behave herself if need be.

"Why do you do that?" Brett asked.

Turning to his older brother, Trevor grinned. "Do what?"

Brett's intense stare didn't waver. "Treat her like that. Mindy's a good girl. She doesn't need someone like you ruining her."

Trevor laughed. "Brother dear, she was ruined long before I met her. I give her a bit of love. Everybody needs love."

"You don't love anyone but yourself," said Brett.

"At least I can get women in my bed and am not a self-imposed monk," Trevor shot back.

"You are such an ass." Brett stood and stomped toward the bar, scattering half-drunk cowboys in his wake.

"Uncle Trevor, that wasn't very nice," Noah piped in.

Shit, he'd forgotten the boy was even there. Noah, at twenty, was his sister Nicky's adopted son. Still growing into his long lanky frame, he had his brother-in-law's intense stare and his sister's propensity for speaking her mind. He stood behind Trevor, his thumbs hooked into his waistband. With a shake of his head, Noah pulled a chair out and straddled it, leaning his arms on the back, his brown-eyed gaze slightly accusing.

"Brett's too damn serious, Noah. Somebody needs to pull the stick out of his ass," Trevor groused with a twinge of guilt.

Noah shrugged. "Still wasn't nice. Uncle Brett means well."

Probably true, but he was always sticking his nose in Trevor's business. As a big brother, Brett was judgmental and every once in a while needed his nose tweaked.

"He'll get over it. Now, what about you, boy?" Trevor cocked one eyebrow.

Noah's cheeks colored, a typical reaction. "I'm not a boy. I'll be twenty-one in a few months."

"You need to get you a woman, Noah. I know one or two who can teach you a few things." Trevor figured every man needed a skilled woman to introduce him to the sins of the flesh.

"No, thanks. I'll find my own way."

"It's your choice, kid. I personally have never let an opportunity to experience a little bed play slip through my fingers." Trevor waggled his eyebrows until Noah laughed.

"Don't poison his mind, Trevor." Brett sat down with a thump and two fresh beers. As Trevor reached for one, Brett handed it to Noah. Noah grinned and lifted his mug in salute.

"Cheers."

Brett clinked his glass with Noah's and gave Trevor a biting smirk.

"Fine, I'll get my own." Jesus, he sounded petulant to his own ears. Dammit, he was thirty-two years old, not twelve. With a shrug, he walked toward the bar and glanced at the poker game going on in the back. A game he hadn't been invited to participate in by the owner of the saloon, Marcus Rollins.

The bartender, Mike, poured him another foamy brew. "If you're interested in playing again, Trevor, I have to ask Mr. Rollins first. You know he hasn't forgiven you for the last time you cleaned his clock."

Trevor slapped down two bits and grinned. "Not my fault if he doesn't know how to play cards."

Mike's furry black eyebrows drew down in a frown, which pulled his thinning corkscrew hair that much closer to his big forehead. "Be careful, Malloy, one of these days you're going to play against someone who will kick your ass from here to next week."

"Don't worry, Mike. It'll never happen." Trevor sipped his beer and watched the poker action. His palms itched to hold the precious cards in his hands. Poker, aside from women, was his passion in life. He was, hands down, the best player in Cheshire. Too bad no one let him play anymore. He'd have to find his pleasure elsewhere.

"What time is Mindy finished tonight?" Trevor asked.

ꟹ

Trevor Malloy loved women in all shapes and sizes. Blondes, brunettes, redheads, tall, short, medium, skinny, voluptuous or plump. They all held an appeal for him and he had feasted on the banquet of feminine opportunity all his adult life.

He didn't quite understand why his brothers chose to get married. The banquet became a one-course meal and where was the fun in that? When his oldest brother Raymond married Lily a month ago, Trevor felt the stirrings of *something*. Exactly what, he couldn't explain, but it was there. Lily was an amazing woman with the strength, character and fortitude of ten men—not to mention she was incredibly sexy.

Alas, Lily chose the sourpuss Ray. Trevor would never understand that since his brother was the unhappiest, foul-tempered person on the planet. Perhaps Lily was moved by pity? Either way, done was done. They were good and married, which left Trevor uneasy and restless.

Ever since meeting Lily, he'd been unsatisfied with his usual playmates. Widow Victoria Benson still had her skills. She pulled him in at lunchtime for a quick tussle when he was in town. Patsy at the milliner knew what to do with rope and twine. Then there was sweet Mindy at the saloon—she was about his favorite. When that long hair wrapped around his heated flesh, Trevor was in heaven.

The night before he'd met up with Mindy after work and they'd had a good time. Not a great time, but good. For some reason, the intensity he normally felt with her was missing. Oh, he enjoyed himself all right, but it felt...off.

He blamed his brothers and sister. Their wedded bliss spoiled his fun. They were constantly kissing, hugging and touching—made a body wonder what all the fuss was about. Then there were his parents. Ugh. It seemed that everyone but Brett and Noah was sparking in the Malloy household.

"Hey, Trevor." Ethan walked into the great room and sat at the table opposite him. He helped himself to a biscuit and a cup of coffee. From the look on his face, he had something to say and Trevor could bet it wasn't good news.

"You gonna say what you came to say or sit there and feed your face all day?"

Ethan grinned. The second oldest, he was the brother who married first, a lovely half-Indian woman named Bonita who was too good for a ballbuster like Ethan. He had their baby brother Jack's blue eyes and a sharp wit that often left his opponent bloody.

"I need you to help Pa with breaking the new horses."

"I'm checking the line fences, you can do the breaking." Trevor wasn't about to do both. That was a lot of work for one man—too much.

Ethan chewed for a minute. "I can't. Pa told me to talk to you."

"I knew it!" Trevor shouted. "All of you married men constantly push your chores on me. I'm sick of it. You were tagged to help Pa so do it yourself."

Trevor pushed away from the table and rose.

"Don't you even want to know why I can't help?" Ethan said around the biscuit in his mouth. "Or are you too busy thinking about how sore you'll be from riding in the saddle, little brother?"

"No. I don't give a shit." He stalked out of the room and snatched his hat from the peg by the door. While he was adjusting it, his father, John, came around the corner from his study and grabbed Trevor's arm.

"You've no call to speak to Ethan like that."

"Pa, I ain't gonna do his work anymore. I've got enough to do during the day as it is riding the damn line fences. If Ethan wants to trade that job with me, then I'll help with the breaking. Brett and I always get stuck with the shit jobs out on the range, in the cold, away from the warm fire and a warm woman. For once, I'd like to stick close to home." Trevor's temper bubbled within him. He wasn't one to get angry easily, but somehow Ethan's request sent him over the edge.

John narrowed his gaze. "You spend too much time thinking about yourself, Trevor. Sometimes family comes first."

That one hurt. Trevor was devoted to his family, always put them above everything else. He shook off his father's hand and yanked open the door. The damp stickiness of the morning slapped at him as he stomped outside.

"Come back here, Trevor!"

Trevor ignored his father's command and kept walking without even thinking about where he was going. He saddled his horse in minutes and led him outside, determined to be anywhere but there.

"Where the hell are you going?" Brett's voice rang out.

Trevor, one foot in the stirrup, turned to look at him. "Away from here."

"There's a lot of work to do today, Trevor. It's not the time to go hunting one of your conquests no matter how horny you are." Brett set the pitchfork against the stall door. "I've been mucking stalls for an hour while you sat on your ass inside.

Now you think you're leaving?" He took off his gloves and tucked them into the back of his waistband. "Think again."

Jesus please us, now Brett was going to give him shit. With a sigh, Trevor pulled his boot out of the stirrup and faced his brother. "Ethan just tried to shove off his breaking duty on me."

"So? You don't have a wife at home who keeps getting sick. Ethan's trying to take care of her and do his own branding. You and I are the only fools left on this ranch without a woman to go home to." Brett sounded angry, which was about the only time Trevor heard more than four words come from Brett's mouth.

"Don't preach at me, Brett. I know exactly what my life is like."

Brett snorted. "Your life is about pleasure and how much of it you can find."

"Who are you to judge me?" Trevor stepped toward him, anger and frustration making him see red. "You probably never even fucked a woman before."

He barely saw Brett move, but he certainly felt the hammer fist slam into his jaw. His ass hit the ground so hard, his teeth vibrated.

"I'm sick of your shitty attitude and of you thinking about yourself, Trevor. Grow up." Brett grabbed the pitchfork and disappeared back into the barn.

Trevor's lip throbbed, his ass hurt, and worst of all, his heart hurt. Everyone in his family seemed to think Trevor was there to serve their needs, fill in the gaps wherever and whenever they appeared. Just because he didn't have a wife of his own didn't mean he had no life.

After wiping the muck off his rear end, he mounted his horse, Silver, and galloped away from the ranch. Away from the pressures of being a Malloy, from the constant press of his family. He hoped one of his lady friends was available because Trevor needed a release.

ꟷꟷ

A sharp slap to his arm woke Trevor. His tongue felt like a flannel shirt and his eyes refused to open. Then a headache waved hello. Loudly.

"Wake up! Jesus, you sleep like the dead, Trevor!" a hissy feminine voice complained with earsplitting attitude.

"Wha-?" was all he could manage.

"Your brothers are downstairs and look about ready to tear this place apart looking for you."

Another shake to the shoulder and a pinch under his arm had Trevor sitting up in bed with a growl. The room spun and he had to grab the bed to keep from falling out of it. He focused on the frowning redhead in front of him.

"Millie? Where's Mindy?"

She slapped him so hard he saw stars. "Trevor Malloy, that's the last time I let you into my bed. I can't believe you just asked me that." With an insulted huff, she flounced over to the wall and slipped a pink robe on. "I hope they kick the crap out of you."

She slammed the door behind her and the frame rattled right along with his brains. Trevor covered his eyes with his hands and focused on breathing and trying to make his mind function. What the hell happened? How did he end up in Millie's bed? The night before was hazy, but he did remember showing up at the saloon before they were open and convincing Mike to let him in. He ate and drank, then drank and drank and drank.

That's where he missed something. In fact, lots of somethings. He must've cajoled Millie into bedding him, enjoyed himself, all without a wisp of remembering it. Dammit.

"Trevor!" Ethan's shout brought him back to reality with a crash. The door swung open and he stood there, with Brett and a smug-looking Millie. Heartless wench.

"Not so loud, Ethan. Hell, they can probably hear you in Laramie." Trevor swung his legs over the bed and realized he was buck naked. A cursory glance around the floor didn't reveal the location of his clothes.

"I don't give a shit who can hear me. You've been gone for two goddamn days without a word. Mama is worried sick and Pa's ready to skin you alive." Ethan stepped into the room and put his hands on his hips with a glare cold enough to spring icicles in July.

"Two days?" That just wasn't possible. "It's Tuesday, isn't it?"

"No, you idiot. It's Thursday. You've already missed two days of the chores. Brett and I decided we needed to drag your sorry butt home. Now get up." He stalked toward the bed and Trevor jumped up, fists raised.

No way in hell he was going to let his brother pull him out of the saloon without a stitch on. "Where are my clothes, Millie?"

She shrugged and raised one eyebrow. "Maybe they're in Mindy's room." With a snicker, she was gone.

Shit.

"Help me look for my clothes." He bent down and ended up on his ass when the floor tilted beneath him. Definitely couldn't do that again. Fortunately, he spotted his britches under the bed and grabbed them. He pulled himself up, or at least tried to. After the third time he fell back on the floor, Brett yanked him up and slammed him onto the bed.

The look in his eyes was fiercer than Trevor had ever seen. It almost scared him.

"You're a disgrace to the Malloy name."

Trevor stared at him, disbelieving that his brother, his closest brother and best friend, would say that to him.

"Jesus, Brett, that hurt."

"Good. Now get dressed."

With a clanging head and cottony mouth, Trevor fumbled through putting his clothes on. He kept an eye on a frowning Brett and Ethan who stood with his fists clenched. Life was too short to be so serious.

"Why are you so damn angry?" Trevor muttered.

Ethan stepped closer and Trevor scrambled to finish buttoning his trousers. "Because you keep shirking your duties at home. Then they fall to the rest of us. Brett's the only other one under Pa's roof and he does twice the work you do. You're lazy, Trevor, and I'm sick of it."

"Hell, Ethan, why don't you tell me how you really feel?" Trevor's hackles were up and his defense mechanisms reared their ugly heads. "Life at home not a bed of roses with Bonita?"

Oh, shit, he knew he'd gone too far when another fist blurred in front of his grainy eyes. *Pow.* On the floor again, this time with a bleeding nose and a loose tooth. Why the hell did his brothers keep hitting him?

"Get your sorry ass up and back home!" Ethan stomped out of the room and slammed the door so hard, one of the hinge pins popped out.

"You shouldn't have brought his wife into this, stupid." Brett shook his head. "Bad enough you were sleeping with whores in the middle of the morning."

"Shut up, Brett." Trevor picked up Millie's silky drawers from the floor and pressed it to his nose to staunch the bleeding. Served her right to have her things ruined after she'd served him up like eggs on a plate to his brothers.

He figured the day couldn't get much worse.

ꙮ

As soon as Trevor walked, or rather stumbled, through the front door of the Malloy family ranch house, he knew he was in trouble. The air was so thick, he imagined he could slice it with a knife.

"Where the hell have you been?" His oldest brother Ray's voice was like a hatchet through his head.

"I was celebrating your nuptials." Trevor thought he hung up his hat on the third try, but somehow it ended up on the floor.

Ray stepped into his line of vision, an intense look in his eyes. Trevor felt a smidge of fear, but then it was gone. He was too old to be afraid of his big brothers. All the Malloy men had similar features with wavy brownish-red hair, the only difference was the eye color, shades of blue or green. Ray seemed to have received the lion's share of persnickety though.

"I got married a month ago, smartass."

Oh, and didn't Trevor know that all too well. Lily was a hell of a woman, too good for Mr. Pickle Puss.

"I was so happy for you I couldn't stop celebrating." Trevor grinned and tried to move past Ray. That was his first mistake.

Within a second, he was slammed into the wall with enough force to shake the house. Ray fisted Trevor's shirt and held him up off the floor. He didn't even want to imagine the strength in Ray's hands to hold up a two-hundred-pound man.

"You fucked up the ranch schedule with your whoring and drinking. We're behind and that makes all of us pay. Your lazy ass has cost us a lot of money and it's coming out of your wages."

Trevor tried to dislodge Ray's hand. Unsuccessfully. "What wages? I get forty dollars a month like every other cowpoke. Why should I kill myself for that? I needed some time off so I took it."

Ray shook him and Trevor's stomach did a somersault. "Now was not the time, you idiot."

"It's never the time." A welling of anger started somewhere near his toes and picked up resentment along the way. "I don't get days off, not even Sundays. I work and work and work and for what? For enough to buy a few whores and some beers, barely enough to keep my tack in good shape."

Ray let him slide down the wall and continued to glare. "You're a selfish little shit."

Trevor never knew what possessed him, but he laid out Ray with a roundhouse punch. "I am tired of being called names and I'm tired of being a Malloy. I quit!"

As Ray lay on the floor rubbing his jaw, Trevor grabbed his hat and stormed out the door. He heard someone call his name from near the corral but he kept on walking. After slamming into the bunkhouse, he took his saddlebags and gear, then without a word to the open-mouthed hands playing poker, he left.

Fortunately his horse was still saddled—sometimes being lazy had its advantages. He slung his saddlebags up and mounted, the anger coursing through him. A hand on his leg stopped him.

"What's happening, Trevor?"

He stared down into his mother's green eyes. Francesca Malloy remained beautiful at sixty-something. A strong woman who never let any of her six sons take advantage of her, she only asked for loyalty and love. Guilt pricked Trevor's conscience but he ignored it for the fury in his heart.

"I'm leaving, Mama. I need to get away from here, away from being a Malloy."

She nodded, understanding in her gaze. "How long will you be gone?"

"I don't know. A while." He didn't want to think past leaving, and he really, really needed to go before his laziness overtook his impetuous anger.

"Where are you going?" Her questions, while simple, were not.

Trevor thought for a moment. "I'm headed to Cheyenne. From there, I don't know. Maybe I'll go see Malcolm and Leigh in Texas."

Francesca closed her eyes and dropped her chin to her chest. When she looked up at him again, Trevor was startled to see a sheen of tears in her eyes. "Just let me know you're okay."

The one thing any Malloy could count on was Mama. She accepted them all for whom and what they were, regardless of choices. Trevor was no fool. If he dismounted, he'd never leave. She had that much power.

"I will. Don't worry. I'll be fine—I can play my way. You know how good I am at poker." He had to tell her something, might as well make it a good one.

"Of course I'll worry. Keep safe, Trevor. I love you." She patted his leg and stepped back.

With a tip of his hat and a nod, Trevor turned his horse toward the road. Toward freedom. The spur of the moment idea to play poker wound its way through his head and suddenly, Trevor had a plan. He'd become a professional gambler, at least for a while. No more cow shit and horse kicks. Getting drunk and whoring for two days was the best thing he could've done.

Opportunity knocked.

Chapter Two

"Escort him out, Dustin." Adelaide Burns surveyed the drunken cowboy drooling over his hand of cards and waved her hand in the direction of the bartender. "He's had enough."

With a heave and a grunt, the seat was emptied, then immediately filled by a bright-eyed boy who didn't appear old enough to shave. The reflection of his smile could have blinded someone. What a greenhorn. Adelaide figured he just got his first pay and came to town to gamble it into a fortune. This little brown-haired baby wanted to play and thought a female dealer an easy mark.

Most folks saw only the exterior shell of Adelaide—the corkscrew red hair, the hazel eyes, the freckles on her nose and the generous bosom that filled out her shirt nicely. They never looked past that and therefore, judged solely on what they saw. They didn't bother to ask who she was, what she was doing, or why she was there.

Townspeople knew Adelaide owned the Last Chance Saloon, but the cowpokes and drifters didn't. They also didn't realize Adelaide was a champion poker player who had made her money in cards, enough to buy the saloon and live as she pleased. Life was good for the most part.

She didn't look at the cards as she shuffled them, the movement a natural extension of her hands. Instead, she monitored the five men at the table, and kept an ear out for anything else going on. It was a quiet Thursday night with only a few rumblings of the chaos to come on Friday when the cowpokes hit town.

"Five card draw, deuces are wild. Minimum bet is one dollar. Ante up, fellas." After the last man threw his dollar into the pot, Adelaide dealt the cards with her normal lightning speed. The baby-faced kid gulped and picked up his cards like he expected them to bite.

"What's your name, sweetheart?" she asked him.

"Brian. Brian Muldoon, ma'am." His voice hadn't really changed yet either.

"Oh, don't call me ma'am. It makes me feel a hundred years old. You can call me Miss Adelaide." She arranged her cards in her hands then glanced up. "You play this one hand, Brian, then you think about how well you played before you play another one. No shame in heading for the whiskey instead of the cards." She didn't want to take *all* his money.

"O-okay." He licked his lips and focused on the cards he gripped tightly enough to curl. A bead of sweat trickled down his peach-fuzzed cheek.

"Bet's to you, Curtis." Adelaide kept the play going, watching Brian as he considered his cards with a furrowed brow before meeting the bet.

After another round of raising the bet, Brian's face was a little peaked. Adelaide waited for the chips to fall, so to speak. When Parker called, only three players remained in the hand, Parker, Adelaide and baby Brian. Parker laid down two pair, tens high. Brian cleared his throat and showed his hand—three little ladies, which impressed Adelaide. However, she would have no self-respect if she lost a hand to a greenhorn like Brian.

"Sorry, sweetheart, but a straight beats your three queens." With a wink, she showed him her cards. Ignoring the crestfallen look on his sweet face, Adelaide focused on her winnings. His gaze followed her hands as she pulled the pot toward her, a modest pot to be sure, but probably a month's pay to the boy.

After arranging the coins and tucking the bills in a safe place, she gathered the cards and started shuffling again. "You in, Brian?"

Brian appeared entranced by her hands as she shuffled. Curtis, bless his crotchety old self, elbowed him. "You in or out, boy? We ain't got all night for you to stare at them cards or them tits."

The boy glanced up at Adelaide and she cocked one eyebrow. "The bar is right behind you. Dustin would be happy to pour you a drink of your choice, on me."

That was apparently all he needed to hear. With a grin, he tipped his hat and left the table.

"Miss Adelaide! Why the hell did you do that? We coulda taken that boy for every penny," Curtis groused.

"Because we didn't need to. He just lost ten dollars in that hand, probably a quarter of his pay this month. No call to let the boy starve, is there?" Adelaide blessed him with a smile—a feat that got harder and harder to do each day Buster McGee messed with her business.

Curtis harrumphed. "Okay, then, let's play."

"You're a good man, Curtis." She patted his hand.

"Don't get all mushy on me, otherwise I might think you're a female." Apparently the gray-haired old prospector still had the ability to blush. Adelaide bit her lip to stifle the laugh burbling in her throat.

"Ante up."

ꕥ

Trevor stopped his horse on the outskirts of the main street in Cheyenne. Busy, but not bustling busy, exactly where he wanted to start his new career. Two saloons sat on either side of him. One was the Silver Spittoon, the other the Last Chance. He surveyed the horseflesh tied up outside and determined the Last Chance had better clientele.

A small hotel sat next door, convenient for his purposes. He tied up the gelding then headed to the hotel to check in. Trevor wasn't stupid enough to walk into a saloon with every cent he owned in his pocket. God only knew what kind of cheaters he'd find within its walls. Sometimes even the dealers cheated.

With his saddlebags slung over one shoulder, he stepped into the hotel to make arrangements for a room. The clerk insisted on being paid up-front. Trevor planned on staying one week—long enough to make money to fund the rest of his trip to Texas. He counted out fourteen dollars and handed it to the bespectacled clerk.

"I expect a hot bath every day and at least one meal included for that price."

"Yes, sir, that's included. The water might still be warm upstairs if'n you want a bath now." He pointed toward the stairs and handed Trevor a key.

Trevor thanked the clerk and walked upstairs to his room. A bath sounded pretty good, but he really wanted to get acquainted with the saloons and the poker action. He made sure there were no bugs in his bed before dropping his gear off.

Nothing like scratching the night away in someone else's mess. He was pleasantly surprised to find the hotel was clean—they must be going after all the travelers coming in on the railroad now that service was picking up.

Trevor emerged into the evening air and took a deep breath. It smelled like success. Sweet and pungent. With a chuckle, he headed into the Last Chance Saloon.

The saloon didn't have any dancing girls, but there were nicely shaped serving gals. He winked at two of them while sauntering toward the bar—they both giggled and winked back. Good sign. The bar itself wasn't new, but it was well taken care of with brass rails top and bottom, and stools that had held more than a few asses. The bartender was a big dark-haired man with a handlebar mustache and a glare that could curdle milk.

Trevor smiled and headed for the bar, trying to keep his eyes averted from the tables toward the back where the poker action was. No music played and an air of relaxed camaraderie filled the saloon. That was also good news. Happy people played poker with better attitudes and there was less chance of a sore loser. Especially one with a gun.

"Evenin'," Trevor said as he sat at the bar. "Beer, please."

The bartender stared at him hard before nodding and setting a mug of beer in front of Trevor. "Four bits."

Steep price for beer, but Trevor set his money down and thanked the grumpy bartender. With one last glare, the man went back to his chore of wiping glasses. Trying not to look like he was spying, Trevor slowly turned and faced the saloon.

There were six tables, two of which had poker games in play. Four or five people sat at each of the poker tables, including a dealer at each one. One of the dealers was a curvy redhead with tits that literally made his mouth water.

Very interesting. A female dealer with hands as fast as greased lightning. She'd obviously been taught by someone with skills. Trevor had never seen a dealer quite like her before and his dick certainly appreciated her as well. Pouty full lips, framed by a pixie nose, freckle-splashed complexion, incredible sunset red hair and eyes that appeared sharper than his knife.

She glanced his way and then turned back to the table without so much as a twitch. Trevor wasn't sure if he should be insulted or not. He wasn't vain by any means, but most women looked at him twice. He'd been blessed with the best looks of the Malloy brothers, which was a fact he accepted at the age of ten when Mary Lou Harris kissed him behind the barn. That's when he realized his looks could bring him untold gifts from women, and not the kind you could necessarily buy.

Trevor sipped his beer and watched the poker game as closely as he could without appearing like he was watching. He wanted to play a hand or two that evening, and there was no need to look anxious. Casual interest, casual game. That was the ticket.

Now all he needed to do was charm the lady dealer and he had it made.

ꕥ

The stranger was, quite simply, stunning. Adelaide noticed him immediately and felt a hard kick of appreciation in her gut for his appearance. With wavy reddish-brown hair and a smile that could melt butter, he sat at the bar and watched, pretending that he wasn't watching.

Adelaide spotted poker players within a minute—this one should have had gambler written on his forehead in grease pencil. Other than his looks, she didn't notice any other redeeming qualities. Gamblers had them in short supply.

When Parker and Curtis left for supper, the stranger stood, stretched, then picked up his beer and ambled over to the table. A long-legged gait, easy movements showing he was comfortable in his skin. With a devastating grin, he gestured to the open chair across from her.

"May I?"

Oh, Lord have mercy. The deep timbre of his voice sent skitters down her skin and made her nipples tighten like bowstrings. Adelaide had a brief moment of imagining that voice whispering dark, sexy words in her ear before she squelched that particular fantasy and sent it packing. She'd sworn off handsome, smooth-talking men a long time ago, so this one didn't stand a chance in hell of getting into her bed, much less her heart.

"Chair's open if you're wanting to play, stranger. One dollar ante, five card draw, wild cards are dealer's choice. You in?" She kept shuffling the deck to maintain focus on what she was doing. His looks were distracting.

"Thank you kindly, pretty lady."

Well, that dampened her unusual arousal, not completely, but a lot. She hated nonsensical shit like that. What was the point of that compliment? Did he honestly think she'd be so flattered that she'd forget how to deal cards? Just another fool trying the "I'm so handsome, won't you fall into my arms" routine she'd heard so many times.

"No thanks required, just the money. Five card draw, threes and sixes are wild. Ante up, fellas."

With four players left, the cards moved more quickly. Adelaide kept her eyes trained on the flirtatious stranger and his charming self. She damn well tried not to look at his long-fingered hands, at the way he held the cards and caressed the edges. She just knew those fingers had an enormous amount of talent for things other than playing cards.

Focus, Adelaide. Don't let 'em distract you. Remember, you hold the cards.

Her grandfather's voice echoed in her ear. He'd taught her everything he knew about cards, and about life. She'd always followed his advice and it never steered her wrong.

Everyone took three cards, except Handsome. He took only one, with a wink, no less. Adelaide cocked an eyebrow and smirked. She received a chuckle in response.

"I can't help myself. Every time I see a pretty lady, I just lose my head," he said as he met the raise and flashed those pearly whites again.

"I might lose my supper if you're not careful." Adelaide finally looked at her cards when she realized the bet was to her. "See your five, raise you five."

"What's your name, darlin'?"

She'd give him his druthers; he didn't give up easily. "You may call me Miss Adelaide."

"Mmmm, Red...that fits perfectly. I'm Trevor Malloy."

"You're holding up the game, Trevor Malloy. See the bet or fold." Adelaide refused to give in to the stranger's charms.

With another chuckle, Trevor saw the bet and called. She wasn't surprised to find he had three tens in his hand and took the pot. Then took the next two hands with a guileless grin and a shrug. The gambling cowboy definitely knew what he was doing. Too bad he had no idea who he was playing against.

Adelaide hated to lose, no ifs, ands or buts. Especially to someone she didn't respect like silver-tongued cowboys. She was done playing—it was time to show sweet cheeks what a real gambler could do.

ꙮ

"You in or out, Trevor?"

Red's voice cut through his panic long enough to actually hear what she said. Trevor's clammy palms barely held onto his cards. This couldn't be happening to him. It just couldn't.

Perhaps it was a nightmare instead.

He wasn't sure what time it was—probably close to three in the morning. The four people left in the saloon all huddled around the table where Trevor sat facing the red-haired demon witch.

"How much is in that pot now?" he asked while wiping his eyes with one hand.

She sifted through the pile. "Looks like six thousand or so in cash and coin, and a gold pocket watch."

He had no idea what possessed him to play for stakes so high. He'd been winning, dammit to hell, and winning big. Earlier in the evening, his normal luck with the cards appeared, and he'd turned his two hundred dollars into a thousand in a few hours.

Then he lost a hand, but he kept playing. He lost another, and another. Soon it all became a blur, hours went by without him noticing. Thank God he left a couple hundred dollars in his room. That was at least something.

If he lost this hand, he'd owe this woman five thousand dollars, more than he'd ever had in his lifetime. That was her raise on the pot and he had to meet it or fold.

In this one hand, one goddamn fucking hand, he put everything he had in the pot, and now he had a marker sitting in front of him. A marker he'd just written out for five thousand dollars. Something he'd never done before. Just seeing the paper out of the corner of his eye made his stomach clench.

Trevor focused on the cards, looking again at the flush he held. This was a winning hand—he was damn sure of it. A beautiful array of hearts, six, seven, eight, nine and ten. The only way she could beat him was with a royal flush. There was no way in hell she had one. No way.

"I'm in. Call." He placed the marker on top and immediately wanted to snatch it back. His father would whoop his ass for doing it. But if he won, Lord if he won, he'd be set for cash for at least two years.

He didn't contemplate what would happen if he lost.

As he laid down his cards, the other two men whistled and murmured between them. Trevor met Adelaide's gaze.

She looked at him with raised eyebrows. "I hope you're good for that marker, cowboy."

Trevor smiled weakly. "Of course I am. But you won't need to worry about it. What does the dealer have?" His palms itched to grab the pot and rip the marker into tiny pieces. His heart had taken up residence in his throat.

"I'm afraid I have bad news for you, Trevor Malloy."

Stomach churning, he watched Adelaide lay down a royal flush. Ten of spades, jack of spades, queen of spades, king of spades, and the ace of spades. The card of death.

Holy ever-loving Christ.

"You owe me five thousand dollars." Adelaide held out her hand and Trevor stared helplessly.

What had he done?

Chapter Three

Adelaide tried to feel satisfaction, but a smattering of guilt overrode it. Trevor looked as if he'd been kicked in the head by a horse. Dazed, shocked and disbelieving. She hadn't meant to let the game go that far—she really only wanted to teach him a lesson. He kept pushing and pushing until Adelaide got riled. She wasn't known for keeping her temper in check once it was released. It appeared to be the only part of her that was Irish aside from her hair.

Now she had gone too far with this one. Not only had she taught him a lesson, but she took more money than he had. She was sure of that.

"Boys, why don't y'all go home now. I'll take care of business with Mr. Malloy here."

With a few grumbled curses, they left, leaving her alone with the charming gambler who now owed her a small fortune. Adelaide started stacking the bills and coins, keeping a close eye on the man opposite her.

"I, uh...need a few days to get the money." He smiled, but she could see the panic in his eyes.

"You're a bad liar."

He sighed and ran both hands down his face. "Jesus, woman, I can't believe I lost that hand. I had you dead to rights, where the hell did that royal flush come from?"

"The deck." After she finished neatening the money, she picked up the cards. "What are you trying to say here?"

"You really don't expect me to pay you five thousand dollars, do you?"

She glared at him. Little weasel was trying to renege on his bet. A marker was a marker. "Yes, I do. You don't pay me, Trevor, and we're going to have a big problem."

"You cheated. That's the only explanation." He stood and started pacing around the empty saloon. His boot heels thunked in the silence. "I could not possibly have lost with a flush."

"The hell I cheated. You lost plain and simple. The sooner you accept it, the better. Now, what are we going to do about the money you owe me?" Adelaide's patience began to wear thin.

Trevor stopped and peered at her across the shadows in the saloon. A shiver danced down Adelaide's spine. When he wanted to, he could look downright predatory. She had no doubt that he'd never run into a woman he couldn't charm before. Must be a double shock to not only meet the antithesis of what a woman is expected to be, but to lose a fortune to her.

Adelaide stood and tucked the money into her pockets. Damn it felt good to have them so full, not only that but it jingled when she walked. Gramps would've been proud of her.

"I just don't have that kind of money, Red," he admitted softly. "Is there anything I can do to change your mind?"

The seductive tone to his voice told Adelaide a lot about where Trevor Malloy thought his strength lay. Apparently, if he couldn't charm his way out of a situation, he tried to seduce instead. Sure as shooting wasn't going to work on her though.

"Nope, and you can just tuck that silver tongue of yours back in your mouth. It isn't going to work on me, handsome.

How much money do you have?” She walked over to the bar and helped herself to a shot of the good hooch that Dustin kept down below. Trevor’s expression didn’t change, but he watched her carefully.

“Two hundred.”

Adelaide had a hard time not spitting that prime whiskey across the room. What a goddamn fool. Betting twenty-five times what he had in his pocket on a single game of cards. “Why did you bet so much?”

“I thought I had you beat. I couldn’t lose...”

“But you did and now I have your marker.” She patted her pocket. “And I intend to make you pay every cent that you owe me.”

ᘐᘓ

Trevor led Adelaide back to his hotel room for the rest of the cash he had on hand. The desk clerk barely batted an eye when she went upstairs with him. Perhaps his lady dealer frequented the hotel more than he thought.

He was embarrassed and shocked in the changes over the last twenty-four hours. He’d left home in a huff, plunked down his life savings in a poker game, and was now deeply in debt to a saloon girl turned dealer. His knees were definitely scraping the bottom of the barrel and it was dark and ugly down there.

Opening the door, he ushered her in then followed. She crossed her arms over those magnificent breasts and waited like a statue. The woman had the best poker face he’d ever seen in his life. He emptied the saddlebags on the bed to show her he was telling the truth, then took the small roll of bills and handed it to her.

"This is all of it. Are you sure I can't change your mind about the marker?" He really hoped she'd say yes, but at the same time, already knew she'd say no. Adelaide was a hard-ass.

"No, I won't. You can work it off."

Trevor gazed into her hazel eyes, trying to determine what kind of work she was talking about. "Where would I be working?"

"At the saloon, of course. You do owe five thousand dollars." She chuckled. "I guess it's your last chance, too."

"So do I owe the owner of the saloon five thousand and not you?" Trevor's confusion grew when she laughed. A husky, gut-busting laugh that made her entire face light up. He thought for a moment she was going to slap her knee or snort.

"You have no idea who I am, do you?" Another laugh escaped as she clutched her stomach.

"You're Miss Adelaide. What else do I need to know?"

What in the hell was she talking about?

"I own the saloon, Trevor. It's mine. Lock, stock and barrel. Not only did you lose to a lady, but you lost to the owner. You'll be working off that money under me."

The triumphant gleam in her eye really got under his skin. He wanted to shout and rant, but he didn't because the situation was already as bad as it could be. Acting like an ass would make it worse. The words "under me" kept playing over and over in his mind, conjuring some incredible images in his head of Miss Adelaide's breasts while he was under her.

Panic and stupidity were not good bedfellows. He needed to rein in his libido and keep his dick in his pants. For now anyway.

"What exactly do you want me to do?"

"Gather up your things and come back to the saloon. Until that money is in my hands, you'll be living at the saloon under Dustin's careful eye." She gestured to his saddlebags. "Move along with that, it's late and I'd like to get some sleep tonight before the sun rises."

"Dustin? Is that the bartender with the pleasant grin?" Trevor's sarcasm reared its ugly head as he started stuffing his things back into the saddlebags. What was worse? Telling his parents he was in debt up to his neck on the first day of his independence? Or living under Dustin's careful eye for a year or two?

Looked like hell had come calling and given Trevor two choices that could break him. There was no way he could tell his parents what he'd done, so that narrowed his choice down to one.

Adelaide, the card sharp saloon owner and her strong-arm bartender, Dustin.

With a sigh worthy of any thespian, Trevor picked up his bags and left the hotel room to become the newest employee of the Last Chance Saloon.

Adelaide could have let him go, but she didn't. She couldn't explain why either. Something about Trevor Malloy made her want to be bad, even if it was just a show for him. As they walked back to the saloon, she hid her grin in the gloom of the night. She figured she could get about a month's work out of him before letting him loose. Hopefully with a lesson learned about what not to do in a poker game when you don't have the money to bet.

He obviously didn't have anyone like Gramps to teach him when to fold and when to raise. Perhaps she should take on that task and save him from further humiliation along the path to wherever he was going.

"You headed to somewhere in particular or were you settling in Cheyenne?" she blurted as they stepped back into the saloon.

"Just passing through I guess. I was kind of headed for Texas, but it doesn't matter because no one was expecting me."

Interesting answer—one she wanted more information about, but they arrived at Dustin's door. With surprising speed, Dustin opened the door and assessed the situation immediately.

"The fool gave you a marker, didn't he?"

"Yep, he sure did. That means we have a new employee, Dustin. Make sure he stays put and doesn't get a hankering to skip town on me," Adelaide said.

"No problem." With a glare, he let Trevor into his room.

Trevor turned and looked at Adelaide. "Thanks for giving me the chance to pay you back."

She hadn't expected that and the sincerity in his voice surprised her. "Good night, Trevor."

He inclined his head and stepped further into the room. With a nod to Dustin, Adelaide headed upstairs to her room. She hoped like hell she didn't have dreams of Trevor Malloy.

ꙮ

Trevor lay on his bed, which was actually a few crates covered with a scratchy blanket, and stared at the ceiling. Sleep eluded him although he was more tired than he ever remembered being in his life. The blackness of the night gave way to the gray light of dawn. Dustin slept so quietly, Trevor almost forgot he was there. The big man moved as silently in his sleep as he did awake.

Trevor didn't know what went wrong. Poker had always come easy for him, the natural inclination to know which cards were coming, the ability to read his opponents' faces. Somehow in the Last Chance Saloon, it all went to hell. If only he could figure out why.

Was it Adelaide? He'd never played against a woman before, they'd always been sitting on his lap. Even if she was the best poker player in the world, he shouldn't have lost so badly. He'd been distracted by her. By those innocent-looking freckles and ever-changing eyes.

The question still remained. Why?

He shifted on the bed and was rewarded with a splinter in his ass. Perfect. A whoosh of air was all the warning he had before a foot tried to push him off the crates.

"Time to wake up, Malloy." Dustin stood over him as Trevor dragged his numb ass up off the crates and pulled on his boots. His body protested the lack of sleep but he ignored it. He owed Adelaide a shitload of money and dammit all, he had to pay her back.

Chapter Four

Trevor drank the coffee, which was hot enough to make his eyes water, then dug into a biscuit with relish. Not as good as his Mama's biscuits, but damn tasty. He had to meet the cook at the saloon and find a way to finagle more delicious eats out of her. At least, he hoped it was a her.

While Trevor wolfed down another biscuit, Dustin huffed an impatient breath and snatched the last two biscuits off the plate.

"You eat too much," Dustin grunted.

Trevor laughed. "I'm still hungry. Where's the kitchen?"

Dustin jerked his head toward the right rear door of the saloon. "Back yonder, but don't you be bothering Marybeth."

The tone of his voice suggested that Dustin was very protective of Marybeth.

"I just wanted a little extra food. I know Adelaide wants me to work hard, and I can't do that if I'm hungry." Trevor grinned.

"If you step out of line, I'll pound you into next week, Malloy." Dustin's mustache twitched along with his left eye.

"Don't worry, Dustin. I'm a gentleman." As Trevor headed for the kitchen door, he swore he heard a growl coming from his keeper.

Living under Dustin's thumb wasn't going to be the most pleasant experience of his life. It seemed Dustin had the personality to match his brawn, hard and unyielding. Reminded him a bit of his brother Ray, only bigger and uglier.

As Trevor pushed open the kitchen door, the scent of something sweet and cinnamony tickled his nose. Whoever Marybeth was, she could obviously cook. He poked his head around the door and found a plump, dark-haired woman kneading dough on a butcher block table. The room had a huge black iron stove, a sink with a pump attached and well-stocked shelves.

Her hair was up in a bun held in place by what looked like a stick. Her homespun dress, likely wool, was protected by a white apron.

"Good morning," Trevor said as brightly as he could and stepped into the room.

Without stopping her task, she glanced up at him. "Does Dustin know you're in here?"

Not the friendliest greeting. Obviously Dustin and Marybeth knew each other well enough to have the same social skills.

Trevor didn't move any closer, just sniffed loudly. "That smells so wonderful, I think I'd sell one of my brothers for a taste of it. Some kind of cinnamon cake?"

Marybeth grunted. "Yes, a streusel recipe from my mother." Knead, knead, knead.

"Then no doubt it will be delicious. What is it about mothers that make their cooking the absolute best? I was just saying to myself while eating a flaky, delicious biscuit that it reminded me of my mama's." He leaned against the table and smiled. "Only thing better would've been strawberry jam on top."

Finally a reaction. He swore she smiled, a teeny-tiny one.

"There's jam in the larder."

Trevor looked at the shelves of supplies. "Really? Do you can it yourself?"

"No, we buy it from Widow Bellevue. Not the quality of my mama's, but edible." Marybeth placed the dough in a big bowl and draped a cloth over the top. She put her hands on her hips and looked at him. "I suppose you want another biscuit, then?"

"Ma'am, I would be forever in your debt for another biscuit...especially if there was a piece or two of bacon with it." His stomach rumbled so loud, he almost blushed.

"You the handsome gambler I hear about that's working for Miss Adelaide?" Marybeth asked with narrowed eyes.

"Oh, I don't know about all that. Yes, I'm working for Adelaide, but me, a handsome gambler? I'm just a rancher from up in Cheshire." Trevor sat at the table.

Marybeth snorted and shook her head. "You're a charmer, then, eh? I should've known. I wondered why she didn't have you thrown in jail. Now I know."

He shrugged with a grin. "I can be charming, I admit it."

"Charm the bloomers off lots of gals, I'm sure." She took two biscuits from the stove and put them on a plate with some bacon. After setting the plate in front of Trevor, who waited patiently like the polite boy his mother taught him to be, she retrieved a jar of jam from the myriad of things on the shelves.

Trevor hopped up and went to the stove to pour some coffee. When he handed Marybeth a steaming mug, she raised an eyebrow.

"Definitely a charmer. Don't be trying to work your wiles on me. I'm too old and fat for the likes of you."

Trevor kissed her quickly on her floured cheek. "No one is ever too old to be charmed."

"Oh, go on with you. Eat that food before I take it back."

Marybeth sipped her coffee and kept her jaundiced eye on Trevor as he enjoyed the rest of his breakfast.

ജ്ഞ

Adelaide woke with grainy eyes and a restlessness she hadn't felt in years. Last night's win echoed in her dreams, or rather, Trevor Malloy did. That damned green-eyed gambler and his amazing smile. She hauled herself out of bed with a groan and slipped on her favorite purple silk robe. She needed coffee.

She felt so out of sorts, she was surprised she didn't fall down the steps. When she got closer to the kitchen, she smelled fresh coffee and her mouth watered in anticipation. The door swung open against her hand and Adelaide fell forward.

Straight into Trevor Malloy's arms.

Sweet heavens. Softness met hardness. Calluses met silk. Adelaide's world tilted as she slammed into a man who made her remember life outside her saloon. Remember that she was first and foremost a woman. A woman who had been long without a man.

Her breasts pressed into his chest and his hands landed on her ass.

"Whoa there, little filly," he whispered.

Adelaide shivered as his breath skipped across her skin. Goose bumps ran down her neck, straight to her nipples. Naked beneath the robe, she knew he felt every curve, every inch of her body. His chest was like granite, his hands like hot mitts, his scent filled her.

She breathed deeply, inhaling his essence—a heady mixture of man and a hint of arousal. His or hers, she wasn't sure. Their body heat mingled and moved together. Adelaide was suddenly very, very awake.

"Red?"

Trevor's voice reminded her of just how close they were, and just how unclothed she was.

"Let go of me, Malloy." She pushed at his chest until he released her and helped her stand. His gaze drifted to her breasts, which swung free beneath the purple silk, then to the nipples poking out like floozies waving howdy. She crossed her arms over her chest and glared at him.

"You have work to do. I'm sure Dustin already has a list of chores." She kept her voice as firm as possible, although she felt nearly breathless from the encounter.

"Yes, ma'am. I'm on my way." He held the door open wide so she could come into the kitchen completely. With a cocky salute to her, he blew a kiss to Marybeth and left.

Adelaide took a deep breath and blew it out slowly.

"You watch yourself with that one, Miss Adelaide," Marybeth warned while shaking a wooden spoon.

"Don't worry, I know what I'm doing."

Adelaide ignored the harrumph and went straight for the coffee. She knew exactly what she was doing. Trevor Malloy wasn't about to make her life change one smidge.

Trevor stood outside the kitchen door and tried to control his breathing. What he really wanted to do was huff and puff, but since he knew Adelaide was on the other side of the door, he didn't. He slowly breathed in and out, telling his body to relax. To forget what her body felt like underneath that purple concoction.

Forget? Not likely in this lifetime.

He knew she was curvy, but never imagined she was so soft, so amazingly sexy that his dick woke up with a vengeance. It strained against his trousers as adrenaline pumped through him in waves.

What the hell just happened?

It was a casual touch, something he'd do for anyone who stumbled and yet...it was as far from casual as you could get without being naked. He'd felt her trembling under his touch, even as he trembled beneath hers.

He shook his head like a dog shaking off water from a dunking. His thoughts were jumbled up and he felt off-balance. Odd, that reaction. There was nothing he could do about it except try to ignore it.

For now he had to go work under Master Dustin and see what the day held for him.

ജ്വ

Trevor squinted through the window outside the saloon and concealed his shock at the darkness that peered back. Not just somewhat dark, but pitch dark. His arms and legs felt numb and his brain had long since turned off. He should have known the day would be hard. As a rancher, he was used to hard work, but it was work in the outdoors, honest work on the back of a horse.

This was women's work, or at the least an unskilled person. He actually scrubbed the saloon floor with a brush, then the stairs, and the kitchen. After that chore from hell, he moved onto polishing the banister leading upstairs with oil.

That was all before the worst hit...and he had to wash dishes. He shuddered at the memory of the greasy, slimy plates that he touched. Disgusting. How did women do that every day?

How could he do it every day? The breakfast dishes weren't too bad, the dinner dishes made his skin crawl, but the dinner dishes...they made his gorge rise.

He'd never realized folks could be so disgusting when they ate. Why would someone spit on their plate? Or leave half-chewed steak? Trevor didn't know how he could get through the next year or two paying Adelaide back. One day nearly sent him screaming from the building.

His latest task was sweeping up the floor, a continuous job that kept repeating like that Greek fella Sisyphus who kept rolling the frigging rock up the hill only to have it roll back. The damn morons in the saloon threw peanut shells, spit, snot and every other thing they could get their dirty hands on.

Dang, he surely appreciated his mama so much more. How did she clean up after six boys and one girl?

Trevor swept his pile into the corner by the bar, then turned around and started sweeping again. Part of his problem was the fact that he hadn't slept in two days. Just the thought of a pillow and blanket made him shiver with longing. It also kept him from thinking about Adelaide.

She was watching him. He felt her gaze on his back as she dealt the cards for another night of poker. The flash of the cards as they slid across the table was almost as tempting as Adelaide's breasts. Two items he tried his damnedest to forget pressed against his chest.

"You missed a spot." Dustin's gruff voice broke through Trevor's self-pity.

Trevor sighed and looked at the burly bartender through stinging eyes. "Where? I've swept every goddamn inch of this floor twenty-seven times already."

Dustin smirked. "You like to complain don't you?"

"It beats getting into a fight with you every ten minutes." Trevor started sweeping again.

With a snort, Dustin flicked a peanut shell at him. "That ain't my choice. Miss Adelaide wants you whole so she can get her money's worth out of your gambling hide."

Trevor batted away the peanut shell, then stopped sweeping and stared at the other man. "Are you telling me she told you not to fight with me?"

Dustin shrugged. "Like I said, ain't my choice. Personally, I'd like to kick your ass back to whatever rock you crawled out from under."

Before he knew what he was doing, Trevor had dropped the broom and vaulted across the bar at Dustin. Hoots and hollers erupted around him as he grappled with the big man. He swung and connected with a jaw harder than granite, ignoring the popping in his knuckles.

A well-placed knee earned him a painful charley horse. He flipped around and gained the advantage of being on top. Dustin's bulk didn't allow him to move quickly, but his punches would probably knock teeth and brains loose. Trevor used his agility to block and weave while he tried to beat the living shit out of the bastard below him.

Stars exploded in the back of his head and Trevor fell forward into a surprised-looking Dustin. Blackness arrived like a dark blanket.

Chapter Five

Adelaide glared at Dustin. "Why did you have to do that?"

"I didn't knock him into next week. You did," Dustin said dryly. "That little bugger attacked me. I was defending myself."

She dipped the rag in the water in the basin stained by blood and wrung out the excess. As gently as she could, she cleaned Trevor's scalp wound. When she saw Trevor fighting with Dustin, she reacted without thinking and whacked her new indentured servant with a spittoon. Fortunately it was an empty spittoon, thanks to Trevor.

At least he didn't have tobacco juice and phlegm on him.

"I think he needs stitches." Adelaide carefully spread his hair and examined the oozing gash.

"Good luck getting the doc in here." Dustin snorted. "He lives in McGee's back pocket next to the sheriff."

"Hell, I know that. Damn Mick is making my life hell."

Dustin chuckled. "So says the Mick."

"Shut up." She pulled up Trevor's eyelids. "Let's take him to the empty room upstairs. Can't have him sleeping on crates if we cracked his skull."

"If *you* cracked his skull you mean." Dustin picked up the full-grown Trevor like he was a sack of potatoes and flung him over his broad shoulder. "I don't think it's a good idea to put him in the room next to you. This one has trouble keeping his pants fastened."

Adelaide was well aware of that little tidbit. He flirted with the girls constantly. No matter who it was, or their age or appearance, he smiled and charmed each and every one of them as if they were queen for a day. Adelaide felt a strange pinch of jealousy that he didn't once try to charm her. In fact, he nearly kowtowed to her. Like he'd saved all his real flirtations for the other women and gave her the leftover groveling.

She followed behind Dustin as he carried Trevor up the stairs. Fortunately, there had only been half a dozen customers left and they'd left after the fight. Trevor's head wound started to bleed again and a drop landed close to her shoe. She shuddered at the sight and bent down to wipe it with the wet rag.

"He's bleeding on the floor, Dustin. Turn him upright."

Womp!

Dustin carried Trevor like a babe, his long arms and legs hanging every which way. Adelaide saw his face, relaxed and almost boyish, except for the blood, of course. Damn, she really hadn't meant to hurt him. Guilt danced up and down on her shoulder with sharpened claws. Nearly made her want to release him from his marker.

But not quite.

Something inside her snagged the reins on that thought and halted it in its tracks. She kind of liked having Trevor indebted to her...a kind of perverse satisfaction for all those other gamblers he'd fleeced with his manipulative ways.

Adelaide walked ahead of Dustin on the landing and opened the empty bedroom. She offered accommodations to all the girls who worked the saloon, however she had no sporting girls. If they chose to bring men to their room, it wasn't supposed to be for money or they'd get tossed out on their ass. The room was empty because Rose, one of her regulars, had gotten herself hitched a few weeks ago and Adelaide hadn't replaced her yet.

There weren't any linens on the bed, but at least the mattress was softer than wood. Sort of. Dustin plopped him on the bed so hard, Trevor bounced and Adelaide heard his teeth clack together.

"Dustin! Jesus, you're going to kill him at this rate. Go back downstairs and finish up."

With one last scowl at the unconscious Trevor, Dustin stomped out of the room. Leaving Adelaide alone with the man who made her remember what it felt like to be a woman.

Adelaide retrieved a basin and fresh water from her room, along with a clean rag, a sheet and a lantern. She set the lantern down and lit the wick, casting the room in a golden glow. The shadows danced across his strongly chiseled features, turning him into a mysterious stranger again.

First thing she had to do was get the sheet under him. Well, no, actually she needed to get him undressed first. And she'd sent Dustin downstairs already. She eyed Trevor's large frame and frowned. Sooner started, sooner finished.

His boots came off easily, sliding down off a pair of nicely knitted wool socks. Someone cared about him. Adelaide had refused to allow him to wear a gun while working, so all she had to contend with was his belt and his trousers.

She snorted. Oh, yeah, that's all she had to work with. Ashamed to realize her fingers trembled, Adelaide made quick work of his belt and the buttons on his trousers. Fortunately he wore a union suit under his clothes so she didn't have to be embarrassed by confronting Trevor's manly parts. She couldn't help but notice it did make a nice bulge beneath the cotton.

As she shimmied the pants down his fanny, her face came closer and closer to him. Her imagination and curiosity nearly undid her resolve to leave him in his union suit. She'd wondered what he looked like beneath his clothes, but damned if she'd take advantage of an unconscious man. Especially one she'd nearly killed with a spittoon.

With a deep breath, she spread out the sheet as far as she could, then rolled him on one side, and finished spreading the sheet. By the time he lay on his back again, she was winded. How the hell did Dustin carry him so easily? Trevor Malloy was not a small man.

For the next two hours, Adelaide doctored Trevor's wound as best she could. The blood finally stopped and it looked as if the wound was closing. Perhaps he didn't need stitches after all. She really didn't want to call the doc in—too many questions she didn't want to answer. And a favor she didn't want to owe.

After wrapping a bandage around his head, Adelaide gritted her teeth against an arousal that seemed determined to rear its ugly head. Even after a day of working, Trevor's scent tantalized her. It wasn't any kind of pomade or soap, it was just...him.

She pulled up a chair next to the bed and watched him for a while. Waiting for him to wake up so she could go to bed. Admiring the curve of his cheek, the strength of his chin and the way his lips were slightly parted as if waiting to be kissed.

Adelaide shook her head to clear it. Pretty soon she'd be kissing him and then she'd really be in trouble.

ഇ ഈ

Trevor woke slowly since there seemed to be a clanging in his head that made his ears ring. In fact, it felt like his damn head had split wide open. If he wasn't mistaken, there was a bandage wrapped around it. Hell, he'd done more fighting in the past three days than he could remember doing in the last three years. This time he apparently picked an opponent who could crack his skull.

He tried to open his eyes without much success. The room lay in darkness around him, a world of sound, taste and touch. He noticed the scent of another—musky, yet feminine—surrounding him. Cool hands stroked his face and his dick jumped a country mile.

"Are you awake?" came a feminine voice.

Who the hell was in his bed? And dammit all, why did he not remember another night of loving? Didn't matter if his head hurt, he was going to enjoy this round in the sheets.

Sensing her head near his, he cupped the back of her neck and brought their lips together. She opened her mouth in surprise and Trevor took advantage. Slow, lingering kisses with tongues sliding against each other. He discovered she had a small scar on her lip, and that her front teeth were slightly crooked. He knew she'd had a peppermint and that she could kiss like a courtesan. What he didn't know was her name or what she looked like. It didn't matter in the blessed darkness they existed in.

She tentatively touched his jaw and his hands slid to her hair. Thick, rich hair, he imagined was the color of midnight. A moan escaped from her mouth as their lips fused together. He was as hard as he ever remembered being and the pain in his head faded as his arousal grew. Eyes still closed, he began to explore her.

He trailed kisses along her jaw. When he reached her ear, he nibbled and laved at the lobe. A shudder passed through his lady as she gasped.

"Mmmm, climb on up here, sugar," he whispered.

"I can't." What she said and what she did were two different things. A tall woman with incredible pillowy breasts climbed on top of him, pressing her pussy against his hardened staff. Heat radiated from the contact.

"That feels soooo good." He kissed her neck softly, tasting the skin as he skimmed his hand along her garment.

"I need to taste you." He pulled the fabric, and realized it was a silky robe. Soon the weight of a breast was in his palm, the nipple peaked. He brought it to his mouth and bit gently, ignoring the pain in his head from the motion. She moaned and pressed it deeper into his mouth.

He licked and sucked her while she took her robe off. Her skin was warm and soft beneath his hands. He followed the sweet curve of her spine down to an ass he squeezed, to a set of legs that seemed to go on forever. She was perfectly formed. With a quick motion, she unbuttoned his union suit and released his aching cock.

She leaned forward and settled on top of him. The scorching feel of her nest of curls forced a moan from his throat. God, she felt amazing, hot and sweet.

"Open for me," he whispered against her skin as he switched breasts.

"Yesssss." Her legs spread in welcome and she slid forward. Lord, she was slick with juices, ready for him.

He rubbed the head of his cock up and down coating himself, nudging her clit, teasing both of them. Until he was mindless with want, until she groaned.

"Please." Her simple request came with a desperate note that echoed through his own need.

"Hang on, honey." Trevor shifted beneath her, poised at her entrance, pulsing with need, aching with desire. He slid in an inch and stopped. She was tight, so tight he almost spilled his seed. His partner wiggled and thrust down, which forced a gasp out of him.

"*In.*" She didn't beg, she ordered.

Who was he to refuse?

Trevor thrust upward, following his primal urges to be deeply embedded inside her passage. His eyes crossed with pleasure, his heart stuttered, his pulse pounded through his aching head, but none of it mattered. None of it. Just the feel of the woman atop him.

Perfect.

She rose up high enough that he nearly slipped out, then pushed down again and again. He tried to maintain his control, but he was hanging on by a thread. A very thin thread that was stretched to its limit.

She clenched around him and rode him like an accomplished horsewoman, joining him in a frenzy of slick flesh on flesh. He laved and bit her nipples, while his hands gloried in the feel of her skin. She did the same, squeezing and touching him, scratching and clawing.

His release threatened and he wanted to be sure she found hers. His fingers found her sweet nubbin of pleasure and he flicked it in time with her rhythm. Over and over, together they climbed the mountain of ecstasy. Panting, steaming heat that reached a crescendo within him. Stars sparkled behind his lids as his body spilled its seed.

As the ribbons of bliss twisted through him, she clenched around him like a velvet fist.

"Trevor!" Her hoarse cry felt like a caress, the depth of pleasure apparent.

Trevor realized he was trembling from the force of his release. He pulled her closer to disguise the shaking before he embarrassed himself.

He kissed her, tasting the tang of sweat and sex. She lapped at his tongue and sucked it into her mouth. Incredibly his dick twitched, seemingly getting ready for more, but his head protested any more bed acrobatics.

"You were amazing," he whispered. She slid off and snuggled next to him and he realized she fit perfectly. One of his hands landed on a soft breast that nestled nicely in the palm. Within moments, a peace stole through him, and sleep claimed him.

Adelaide lay beneath Trevor's arm and tingled from the incredible sex they'd just shared. Certainly, she hadn't intended to be with him. Somehow, her brains went out the window when his lips touched her. He tasted so good, so perfect, her body took over.

She knew he must have been experienced. No man looked that good without a slew of women throwing themselves at his feet, and not just soiled doves either. No doubt he had his pick of females throughout his life.

However, she hadn't expected his experience to be beyond her own. To take her to a place where she'd never been, to find a pleasure so incredible she still shook from it.

Trevor could easily become addictive. As it was, Adelaide was having trouble controlling the urge to wake him.

One thing was certain, he could never know how deeply she craved his touch. Adelaide must maintain control.

ꕥ

"Holy shit!" The booming voice echoed through Trevor's head until his eyes watered. "What the hell are you doing buck naked with this...this gambler?"

Trevor focused on the angry-looking Dustin at the foot of his bed, fists clenched and face as red as a beet.

"Relax, Dustin. I didn't hurt her."

"Shut up, you little weasel. Adelaide, what in tarnation were you thinking?"

Adelaide. Adelaide. Adelaide.

That was impossible. It was *not* Adelaide sliding from the warm sheets and putting on a bathrobe. The woman he'd made love to, whose scent still ghosted across his skin. It couldn't be. Trevor turned his head.

Holy hell. Adelaide.

There she was, glorious unbound red hair streaming down her back, her skin marked by whisker burn. By *his* whiskers. He saw the sweet curve of one breast before it was swallowed by the purple silk.

"Adelaide?"

She snapped her gaze to him and must have seen the confusion in his eyes. "Don't worry about it, Malloy."

Worry about it? Hell, he didn't even know about it. How could Adelaide be the woman in his arms, the woman his cock was currently yowling for? She didn't even like him much less want to bed him.

"Get out, Dustin. This doesn't concern you." The steel in her voice was unmistakable. With a murderous scowl aimed at

Trevor, the big man stomped out of the room, slamming the door behind him.

The awkward silence unsettled Trevor. He had no idea what to say to Adelaide. The silver-tongued ladies man was at a loss for words. The world tilted beneath hm.

She sat on the edge of the bed and peeled up the bandage he belatedly realized was still on his head.

"Looks good. The wound is pink and has a nice scab. I thought it might need stitches, but you'll be all right. I see another scar up here near your hairline too." Her fingertip traced the scar from the wound he'd received almost two months ago at Ray's house. A shiver danced under her touch. "Someone else must have wanted to hit you over the head too."

Adelaide smiled and Trevor felt like a deer under a hunter's gun. Sweet heavens, when she smiled her entire face lit and she was stunningly gorgeous. He swallowed hard and opened his mouth to speak, but the words still would not come.

"I didn't mean to hit you so hard. I wanted to get you off Dustin and...well, I'm sorry." She leaned forward and pressed her lips to the scar. Trevor's body heated instantly. The smell of woman, the remembrance of sex and the musk of arousal crowded around him.

She cupped his face and kissed him. "Good morning."

Before he could react, she was gone, striding through the door to leave him alone, with a painful hard-on and a befuddled brain.

Good morning indeed.

Chapter Six

Adelaide sat at the bar and counted last night's take from the poker tables. Close to three thousand dollars total. Friday's were always a good night because all the cowhands came into town to spend their pay. With Monty and Bernard dealing, along with herself, they had three tables available. She'd wrestled with the idea of adding the third dealer for a few months, but now she was glad she had. The extra income helped all of them, especially since she gave the dealers ten percent of the evening's totals.

A callused hand landed on the back of her neck and yanked her backward until she nearly fell off the stool. Adelaide stared up into the foul face of Buster McGee. His strong, thick fingers held her immobile while his dark gaze glittered with malice and what she thought was arousal.

The owner of the saloon across the street, Buster had made it his business to get into her business. The ugly truth was he didn't want her as competition and did everything he could to drive her into the ground. Legal or illegal. With the Union Pacific Railroad building going in, he was damned determined to force her to sell so he could reap the profits of more business in town. A bully, plain and simple.

He obviously underestimated the will of Adelaide Burns. She hadn't caved in nor had she fallen to pieces.

Buster took off his bowler hat and his curly black hair sprang up like a rat's nest.

"Top of the morning to ya, Adelaide." His breath smelled like onions and his teeth resembled them.

"Let go of me," she snapped.

"Not until you hear me out." He glanced around the empty saloon. "Looks like your pet is someplace else so you and me are gonna have a chat."

"You've got to the count of five to let me go or I drill you a new nostril." Adelaide's hand drifted toward her pocket, but another stopped her. Damn, McGee had someone with him. Someone who snatched her derringer before she could reach it. Where the hell was Dustin? He was supposed to be restocking the bar from the storage room.

"I don't think that will be necessary now, Adelaide." He smiled wider.

Adelaide's back screamed in agony at the position she was in, hanging off the stool, her weight held by this bastard's hand. She couldn't move or she'd risk a broken neck. His hold was as tight as iron.

"I told you not to call me that. It's Miss Burns to you."

He chuckled. "All fancy now, are we? I knows where you came from and it ain't no highfalutin' school."

"What the hell do you want?" she spat.

"Cooperation, Adelaide. You need to listen to me and sell this flea-bitten saloon to me."

Adelaide's heart pounded in anger. He thought he could come in here and simply tell her to sell. As if she had no will and would fall at his feet like a simpering sissy.

Not a chance in hell.

She twisted quickly and bit his hand, surprising him. He let out a yelp and loosened his grip. It gave her the opportunity she needed to shimmy out of his grasp and slide down the stool onto the floor. She landed with a thump then rolled out of the way of the stomping feet.

Unfortunately, she didn't get far. One booted foot trapped her unbound hair, yanking her to a halt, and nearly taking it out from the roots. She yelled and started punching the leg attached to the boot.

A sharp slap met her efforts.

ঌ৩

Trevor kept an eye on Adelaide all morning, at least when he could. She seemed to be everywhere, busy doing all her daily tasks with Dustin at her side. He still couldn't come to terms with the fact that he'd slept with Adelaide.

Had amazing sex with her. Sex so incredible he was half-erect just thinking about it. With an annoyed grunt, he went into the kitchen to wash up the breakfast dishes. He actually enjoyed spending time in the kitchen with Marybeth. Reminded him a bit of home, of his mother. He missed her and home, not that he'd admit that to anyone until pain of death or torture. There were a few things a man had to be manly about. One of them was missing his mama.

He put the last load of plates into the soapy water as Marybeth stepped outside to "take care of business". It wasn't until he heard Adelaide yell that he realized something was wrong in the saloon. He slammed out of the kitchen and assessed the situation in a blink.

Two men were holding her down, one of them had his boot on her hair. The other straddled her waist. She struggled and punched at both of them. Trevor felt rage sweep through him like a bonfire.

He yanked the man off her stomach by the collar, earning a choking sound that gave him grim satisfaction. He punched that bastard in the nose, spraying blood everywhere. The second one, a black-haired, scurvy devil, slammed into him with a roundhouse punch to the right side of his jaw. Trevor stumbled, but didn't fall. He ducked to avoid the next punch and landed a blow to the man's flabby paunch.

"Lousy bastards!" Adelaide picked up her favorite spittoon and wielded it like a weapon. "Get out, McGee, or I swear to Christ I'll split your head open."

Trevor knew she meant it. Hell, he still had a headache from his encounter with that damn brass thing.

"Call off your dog." The one he assumed was McGee bared his yellowed teeth at Trevor.

"Only if you take your lackey and get your asses out of my saloon in the next ten seconds." Adelaide looked about ready to do murder. Her eyes glowed with fury and retribution, a veritable warrior goddess.

A twinge of pride for her rang through him. Reminded him a bit of his sister, Nicky, a woman who didn't take shit from any man.

Trevor stood, fists at the ready, until McGee started dragging his companion out of the saloon.

"I'll be back, Adelaide. Don't you be worrying about that," McGee snarled as the door closed behind him.

Trevor's blood rushed through him like a lit fire as he looked for more sons of bitches to pummel. He was frustrated that he'd only gotten a few good punches in. Wasn't much of a fight. Hell, he got more out of one of his brothers when they were drunk. That ass McGee definitely had trouble written across his face.

"What did he want?" Trevor felt his jaw where the idiot had hit him. Slightly swollen, no teeth loosened though. He looked at Adelaide. She stood with her fists clenched, hair dirty, and a mixture of anger, fear and frustration on her face.

"Red?" He stepped toward her, but she didn't answer him. "Are you okay? Did they hurt you?" Trevor reached her side and cupped her cheek until she turned her gaze to his. "Honey, can you hear me?"

"I'm not deaf, Malloy. I'm just angry as hell. How dare he?" She huffed out a breath. "Did you see what that bastard did?"

Trevor noticed a red handprint on her cheek and realized the sound he'd heard was a slap. McGee dared lay his hands on her. A fresh wave of anger whooshed through him and he couldn't stop himself from following that dirty cur. As he headed to the door, Adelaide grabbed his arm.

"Where are you going?"

"I'm gonna pound that son of a bitch into next week."

"No, you won't. This is my fight." She yanked on both his arms. "You leave him to me."

Trevor almost laughed at the absurdity of it. She wanted him to back away from a fight so she could handle it. He touched the mark on her cheek, then leaned forward and kissed it. She sucked in a breath that he felt all the way to his toes.

His mouth followed that breath and his lips landed on hers. The heat of anger gave way to the heat of passion. She wrapped her arms around his neck and pulled him against her.

Perfect.

She fit to him like a glove. Her lips danced and sang with his as she rubbed her breasts against his chest. No longer half-erect, his dick lengthened and hardened against her softness. In another minute, he'd have her back in bed, deliciously naked in his arms.

He licked her lips from one end to the other until she opened her mouth with a sigh and her tongue rasped against his. Oh, *yes*, so hot and wet. Trevor needed to be with her, alone. Adelaide's hands fisted in his hair, pulling him closer. He reached around to cup her breast and found the nipple hard already. Rolling the turgid peak between his thumb and finger, Trevor sucked her lip into his mouth.

"God, heaven...you taste like heaven," he whispered against her mouth.

"You two are like a couple of goddamn rabbits." Dustin's annoyed voice shattered the fog of arousal surrounding them. He set a handful of bottles on the bar with a tinkling thump of glass.

Trevor broke the kiss and stared into Adelaide's befuddled eyes. "Damn, woman, I can't seem to keep my hands off you. What's that all about?"

She pushed away from him. "I expect that's a common occurrence when you're around any woman, Malloy."

Dustin's normally hard expression turned to granite when he caught sight of Adelaide. He grabbed Trevor by the shirt front and pulled him up to his furious face. "What did you do to her?"

Adelaide slapped at his hands. "He didn't do anything, Dustin. It was McGee. Now let him down."

With one last narrow-eyed glare, Dustin let him back to earth. Trevor realized he'd gotten off lucky last night—the big man could have snapped him in half. It was like being held by a three–hundred-pound dragon with rock-hard fists.

"Why was McGee even in here?" Dustin growled.

Adelaide gestured widely with her arms. “The door was open and you weren’t here. How do you think he got in? Magic carpet?”

“No need to be so harsh, Adelaide. You look like someone beat the shit out of you.”

“They were about to. That bastard was standing on her hair while his minion sat on her.” Trevor grew angry again just thinking about it. “I wanted to go pound the daylights out of them, but she wouldn’t let me.” He jerked an accusatory thumb at Adelaide.

Dustin glowered. “I know. She keeps telling me the same thing.”

Both men looked at her with annoyed, “let me be the man” expressions. She burst out laughing, gut-busting laughs that made her bend over and hold her stomach.

“If…you…c-could see…yourselves,” she gasped out between guffaws. “It’s…like s-someone…shrank D-Dustin.”

Trevor glanced at Dustin, then back at Adelaide. “We don’t look anything alike.”

That just sent her off into longer peals of laughter. After she got herself under control, she wiped the tears from her eyes and hiccupped a few times.

“Damn, I needed that.” She shook her head at them, then walked over to Dustin and kissed his cheek. “Thank you for being worried about me. You are the brother I never had.”

When she turned to Trevor, his heart skipped a beat. Adelaide was getting under his skin. He was losing control and he had no idea what to do about it. Dangerous territory since he’d always maintained a sense of being in charge around women. His charm usually did the trick.

She flipped her hair back and a small grin tilted the corner of her mouth. "As for you..." She poked him in the chest. "There's work to be done, so get to it."

With one hard kiss and a shocking squeeze on his ass, she grabbed up her pile of receipts and money and walked into the hallway, out of sight.

"I'm in trouble." Trevor didn't realize he'd spoken it aloud until Dustin chuckled.

"Yep, I reckon you're right about that. Shoulda kept your dick in your pants, cowboy." Dustin went behind the bar and picked up the bottles he'd set down. "Adelaide gets into your blood and there ain't a damn thing you can do to get her out."

ઊଓ

Adelaide stared out the window of her office, trying to make heads or tails out of her confusion. Out of her current state of perpetual arousal that she couldn't shake.

Trevor Malloy had gotten under her skin.

Even hours after the last kiss they'd shared, she could feel him on her. Could still smell his scent, like it had taken up permanent residence in her nose. Adelaide certainly wasn't a virgin, nor inexperienced. She'd had men before, but never one who was constantly on her mind. One who lit up that flare in her heart for something permanent. The "H" word she'd never spoken aloud.

As she put the money in her reticule for a trip to the bank, Adelaide tried to shake off the deep thoughts. They clung like burrs on socks. The added complication of Buster McGee and his increasingly violent threats just contributed to her overall anxiousness. Life had been complicated before Trevor stepped into her saloon. Now, it was doubly so.

She wrapped the reticule string around her wrist and stood. No use staying in the office any longer, she hadn't done a lick of work in the two hours she'd been sitting there. Instead, she'd go to the bank then have lunch down at Mellie's.

Nodding to Dustin on the way out, he growled and shook his head no. She frowned and he frowned harder.

"What?"

"You are not leaving without protection. Wait until I can come with you." His tone didn't invite argument.

"I can't wait. I've got things to do, Dustin. Don't be such a worrywart." She headed for the door, hoping he'd let her go.

No such luck.

She turned to tell him to leave her alone and found Trevor at her elbow. His appearance was unexpected enough to make her mouth drop open.

"Don't you have dishes to do?" she snapped.

"No, they're done and there's no one in here eating lunch yet. I'm coming with you." He herded her toward the door until she dug in her heels to stop him.

"What are you doing?"

"If you don't have the sense of a goose, it's up to me to be your common sense." He tugged harder.

"If I can't go with you, I guess pretty boy is okay. He held his own against McGee this morning anyway." Dustin must have thought he was being helpful, but he just aggravated Adelaide further.

"Look, both of you, I don't need an escort. I'm walking down the street to the bank and then for lunch." With a haughty sniff, she shook off Trevor's arm and stalked out the door.

She knew the second Trevor started following her—he wasn't exactly being stealthy. Like an overgrown dog at her heels, he followed her to the bank, waiting patiently outside. Then when she went into the mercantile, he stood at the door. She took an extremely long time looking at everything just to annoy him. Served him right for being her shadow.

After paying for her purchases, she strolled down the street, peeping at the storefront windows, saying hello to folks and generally being as slow as she could be without actually stopping. The third time she heard him sigh dramatically, Adelaide knew a moment of sweet satisfaction.

She whipped around and pinned him with a glare. "Next time do as I say, not as you please. I don't need you."

"I know you don't, but it makes me feel better to be here for you."

Well, she didn't have a response for that. It was sweet and the kind of mush that made a girl's heart go pitty-pat. Damn Trevor and his silver tongue anyway.

As she stomped off toward Mellie's, her stomach rumbled noisily at the delay for lunch. Adelaide hoped there was still some of the day's special left so she didn't have to settle for canned peaches and bread crusts. The bell over the door tinkled as she walked in. Adelaide deliberately shut the door behind her.

Margaret, the owner's daughter, smiled at her. "Miss Adelaide. You're kind of late for lunch. We've got a bit of the meatloaf left, if'n you're wanting some."

A spinster at forty, Margaret was a sweet lady with sparkling brown eyes, shaggy blonde hair and a rounded figure. She'd been the first to be kind to Adelaide when she first arrived in town. Since then, Adelaide had frequented Mellie's restaurant.

"Meatloaf sounds perfect, Margaret." As Adelaide sat at a small table by the window, she nodded to a couple eating nearby. The bell tinkled again and she knew it was Trevor. She waited for him to come to her table so she could shoo him away.

After a murmured conversation with Margaret, his footsteps didn't lead to her. They led *away* from her. Adelaide knew she shouldn't look to see where he went, but dammit all. He was supposed to be guarding her, right? So where the heck did he go?

After a few minutes, she couldn't stand it any longer. She dropped her napkin and glanced behind her only to see Trevor at a table with someone else.

That someone else was a woman.

She didn't remember actually getting up, but she found herself standing next to the table staring accusingly at Trevor. A man with the most innocent of expressions plastered on his face.

"What's wrong, Miss Adelaide?" he had the nerve to ask.

Adelaide glared at him, then at the hussy at the table. "You will sit with me since I own you, Malloy."

He shrugged. "Anything you say." Trevor stood and bowed to the young woman at the table with her pretty white fluffy dress and blue eyes. "My apologies, Miss Carson, but my employer has requested my attention. Perhaps I'll see you around town?"

"Of course, Mr. Malloy. These things happen." The little princess practically sneered at Adelaide. "I hope to see you soon," she cooed at Trevor.

With a devastating grin that made Adelaide's toes curl and her fingers into claws, Trevor took her elbow and led her back to her table. The heat from his touch notched up her temperature, which simmered from the anger pulsing through her.

He held out her chair and she sat back down, noting that Trevor had impeccable manners, even if he was a cad.

"You are not to flirt or tease or whatever the hell you do with women while in my employment. Is that clear?" Adelaide knew she was snarling but couldn't help it. Her sharp tongue seemed to have taken over her body.

"Absolutely, Miss Adelaide." His gaze never wavered from hers. In the depths, she saw a reflection of her own hunger.

Damn, they were both in trouble.

Chapter Seven

The next week passed quickly. Each day Trevor worked his ass off, each night, he slept like the dead. Interestingly enough, he was allowed to stay in the second-floor bedroom. He expected Dustin to drag him back to the bed of crates, but it didn't happen.

Trevor secretly hoped his new sleeping arrangement was to be near Adelaide for nightly visits. Alas, that hadn't happened either. He woke up each morning with a stiff dick and a grumpy disposition. It had been seven days since Trevor had intimately touched or been touched by a woman. Seven long days. He could have bedded any one of the serving girls—they'd made that clear the first two days. He received the standard winks, bumps, breast brushes and breathy whispers.

None of them came from Adelaide. Unfortunately, she haunted his dreams. An unusual situation Trevor felt unprepared to handle. When had the tables been turned and how did he get into such a mess?

At fifty cents an hour—generous is what she called it—Trevor had a long way to repay five thousand dollars. Even if he worked twenty-four hours a day, it would be well over a year before he achieved that enormous sum. He was stuck, plain and simple, and with a woman who embraced life in all its goodness and its badness. Trevor wasn't used to that and didn't know what to do. He'd never met a woman, other than his sister, who didn't try to make the world a brighter, better place.

To make matters worse, someone had taken a shot at her. Just the memory of it made him break out in a cold sweat.

Trevor had been behind the bar counting the bottles when the tinkling of broken glass was the only warning he had. The air was split by a high-pitched whine followed by a thunk and some splintering wood in the back wall of the saloon.

Adelaide sat at the table, cards scattered on the green cloth in front of her. Trevor practically flew across the saloon and knocked her out of her chair, throwing his body across hers.

"Get down," he ordered when she struggled beneath him.

"What happened?" She sounded a bit dazed.

Trevor had smelled gunpowder and realized it was coming from her hair. The bullet had actually gone through it. His stomach seized and adrenaline flooded his system.

"Goddamn cocksuckers took a shot at you! Son of a bitch!" He glanced up to see a hole in the wall, neatly made by a rifle shot if he wasn't mistaken.

Big feet ran through the saloon, making the floor vibrate beneath Trevor and Adelaide.

"Dustin, check outside. Someone just shot at Adelaide," Trevor shouted from the floor.

Dustin sounded a bit like a bull as he slammed outside. The shooter was likely long gone or running for Colorado after catching sight of Dustin in all his fury. After what seemed like an hour, he came back in and walked to them. He peered over the table with a frown worthy of an award.

"Whoever the son of a bitch was, he's gone. I found the casing across the street in the alley. Bastard took off on a horse, more than likely a rented nag." He popped his knuckles.

Trevor finally let Adelaide up from beneath him and helped her to stand. A little dirty, and a lot confused, she glanced at Trevor, then cocked her head at Dustin.

"Did somebody try to kill me?"

Dustin's features eased and he put his arm around her, leading her away from Trevor. "Yes, Adelaide, they did."

Trevor had wanted to be the one to comfort her, to have his shoulder be the one she rested her head on. Unfortunately, he wasn't that man.

The entire episode had left him shaken for more than one reason. He couldn't sleep for thinking about it.

He'd been a fool. Both in poker and in dealing with Adelaide. What he needed to do was get under her skin, give her sleepless nights and make her pant for him. Something women usually did anyway. There must be something wrong with Adelaide.

Either that or Trevor was losing his touch. That thought alone kept him up. He sat in the saloon, lit only by a single lantern he'd brought downstairs with him. A deck of cards sat comfortably in his hands. Shuffling and reshuffling, he stared into the darkness and wracked his brain for a solution to his problem.

Adelaide.

As if conjured from his thoughts, she appeared on the steps in that damn purple robe. Her delicious unbound breasts swayed beneath the silky fabric as she walked. Her red tresses streamed down her back, seemingly emitting a glow of their own in the shadows.

Trevor drank her in, absorbing the sight and sounds. She worried her bottom lip with her teeth and he couldn't help but focus on them. He wanted her teeth on him, her lips covering his.

Dammit to hell. He was like a green boy with his first crush.

Snap out of it.

When she stepped toward the table, the deck of cards exploded from his hands in a shower of red, black and white. He sighed and rose to pick them up. Adelaide stood behind him and her scent surrounded him, infusing him with the want of a thousand men.

"What do you want, Red?" he ground out, desperate to taste the skin that was inches away from him.

"Not very polite, Malloy." Her husky, sleep-tinged voice caressed his ears.

"I'm not feeling very neighborly right now. Why don't you get your drink and head on back to b—upstairs." He'd nearly said the word "bed", which would have sent his pulse soaring. No need to fan the fire himself. She was doing an excellent job on her own.

"Why are you here?"

"Afraid I'll run? I think I've proven I don't welch on a bet." Trevor had to climb under the table to retrieve the last few cards, startled to notice his hands shaking.

"No, I don't think you'll run." She hooked a hand under his arm and pulled him up. Her hazel eyes seemed deeper in the dead of night, more mysterious, more intense. "I mean, why are you in Cheyenne? Around here you might get shot if you stand by a window. And unless I miss my guess, you have a family somewhere missing you."

She shouldn't have poked that sore spot.

"None of your business, Red." Truth be told, he missed his family, even the pain in his ass, big brother, Ray. He especially missed all his nieces and nephews. And Brett. He hadn't contacted them because of embarrassment over his current situation. Soon he'd send a letter to his mama to let her know he was all right.

Adelaide cupped his cheek and his whiskers rasped against the softness of her palm. "You're a mystery, Trevor. One that I can't puzzle out."

She'd called him Trevor for the first time. Holy hell. That was the final straw. With a small yank, she tumbled into his arms and his body screamed in victory. Her breasts pillowed against his chest, her pussy a lovely cleft for his hardening staff.

Trevor took Adelaide's face in his hands, noticed her dilated pupils and the small breaths puffing in and out of her mouth. When his gaze settled on her lips, she licked them and that was that.

His mouth descended on hers in a rush. Incredibly soft lips moved restlessly against his, rubbing and nipping. Her mouth opened like a flower in spring, the hot recesses welcoming the plunder. Tongues dancing, sucking and tangling with each other.

The heat between them rose quickly, turning Trevor into a desperate man. He needed to touch her skin, to feel her.

"Red...I can't... Don't say no." He sounded like a complete idiot, but he couldn't even speak coherently so great was his hunger for her.

"Sit," she commanded after backing him up to a chair. His ass landed with a thump. As he watched with barely controlled urges, she unbelted her robe and let it fall open. Her raspberry-colored nipples were level with his mouth. Time for a taste.

Trevor pulled her close and his mouth latched onto one beautiful breast. Sweet, sweet honey of the gods. He licked and sucked her, bringing the nipple to a rigid peak. As he rubbed his lips against her soft nipple, his hand tweaked the other side.

"God you taste good," he whispered. "Good enough to eat."

When he bit her nipple, she yelped. "What are you doing?"

"Mmmmm...tasting you. And I'm still hungry."

In a frenzy of arousal the likes of which he'd never felt, Trevor dropped to his knees and pushed his face between her legs. Her musky scent met his questing mouth. He licked her from top to bottom, eliciting a long groan that made him grow an inch longer.

"Open for me, honey. Please," he nearly begged.

Her legs shifted open a few more inches and he dove forward, eager to bring her pleasure. He spread her nether lips to find her glistening with excitement, ready for him.

"Trevor." Her whisper sounded as desperate as he felt.

"Let me love you, Red." He kissed her, tongue sneaking out to gently lap at her nubbin of pleasure. Caressing and laving her, keeping her on the edge of orgasm, only to fuck her with his tongue until she clenched around him. Then he went back to licking, bringing her clit to a peak as large as her nipple.

Yes.

He sucked her then while his finger slid in and out of her pussy, fucking and sucking. She moved against him in small thrusts, her breath hitching. Trevor glanced up to see her pinching her own nipples and he almost came in his pants.

"That's it, pretend it's me biting you."

When he pushed two fingers inside her and bit her clit, she came so fast Trevor almost didn't catch her after her knees buckled. One arm latched around her waist while his mouth never lost contact with her pulsing core. He continued to lick and suck her until she pulled his head away.

Her eyes glittered in the lamplight. "More. Now."

She indicated the chair and he sat again like an obedient boy. The circulation in his pants was getting to be a problem as his cock grew to monumental proportions. Adelaide straddled him, then reached down and unbuttoned his pants until he sprang free. A gusty sigh escaped when her hands closed around his aching hard-on.

"You're ready for me, then?"

Trevor croaked a laugh. "Another minute and I'll be past you."

She caressed the head and leaned closer to position herself over him. "We can't have that, now can we?"

Like a blind man using his other senses, he felt her coming closer and closer, the heat pouring off him to her or vice versa. He couldn't tell. When his skin met the moist folds of her pussy, he grabbed the chair to keep from impaling her.

With aching slowness, she sank down on him, inch by inch until he was fully sheathed. Surrounded by her scent, by the soft whisper of her robe and the tight warmth of her body, Trevor finally felt at home. Here with her now.

"Sweet Jesus," she breathed.

"Nope, just heaven. Ride me, Red."

Adelaide had amazing powers. She taught him more about how to fuck on a chair than he ever thought possible. Slowly, quickly, with her knees up and down. She could even ride him while he licked her nipples. Thrust met thrust as they rocked together, deeper, harder, faster.

"Come with me," he said in a choked voice.

His hand swept down to rub her clit in circles, matching the pace of his mouth on her nipple. Suck, rub. Suck, rub. Lick, tickle. Lick, tickle.

"Trevor," she cried hoarsely as her fingers dug into his shoulders, rocketing him to the most intense orgasm of his life. Pleasure ricocheted through him from head to toes, tingles following the waves. He held onto her hips as he thrust deep enough to connect them as one.

One body, one soul.

Adelaide shook with a myriad of sensations and feelings, not the least of which was incredible pleasure. She'd just experienced the most amazing sex of her life. On a chair, in the semi-darkness, in her saloon.

Dustin more than likely knew what was going on, but wisely stayed in his room. She'd made enough noise to rouse the neighbors, so no doubt he'd heard her. Adelaide couldn't be quiet when she fucked, it wasn't in her nature. Screaming and moaning and thrashing came naturally. No need to pretend otherwise.

Trevor sat beneath her, his forehead resting on her breastbone. The heated puffs of his breath skittered down her skin to her pussy—to where they were still joined. He filled her completely, with not a smidge of room to spare. Not only that, but the man had a golden tongue, forget silver. He'd pleasured her with his mouth with such skill she hadn't been able to stand up afterwards without assistance.

Even now, she felt weak as a kitten. The edges of his hair had curled in sweaty little ringlets that she longed to play with.

Her hands lay on wide, wide shoulders, unsurprised to note she'd made crescent-shaped marks on the skin with her fingernails. She almost lost her mind in the rush of her orgasm. Not only that, but it was the second of the night and it drained her to the point of exhaustion. It surely drained him.

Adelaide let out a breath that ruffled his hair. She tried to stand, but her energy was totally spent. In fact, she could hardly move.

With a small degree of embarrassment, she cleared her throat. "Um, Trevor? I can't seem to stand up."

He glanced up at her with a wicked grin. "Mmmm, you can't, eh? Well, I'll have to take care of that."

Before she could protest, he'd stood with his arms locked around her ass and his cock still deep inside her. It was the most amazing sensation she'd ever had—akin to riding a horse. The motion as he walked drove him slightly in and out. When he got to the stairs, she moaned as her clit made contact with his pubic bone. With each step, they pushed together over and over. Unbelievably, she was getting aroused again. Ready for him.

Seemingly impossible, but true. She leaned forward and nibbled on his neck, the salty tang of his skin coated her lips. Kissing her way along, she found his ear and licked the shell of it, smiling when he shivered beneath her.

When they got to the top of the stairs, he huffed out a breath. "You're starting something. Gonna finish it?"

They arrived at her door and he stepped inside. The room lay in near blackness and their breaths echoed back at them. Adelaide's heart beat a staccato rhythm against her chest as she waited for him to close the door. When he didn't, she reached behind her and made sure it latched.

"As long as you're not busy." She claimed his mouth, hot and hard, tongues dueling and dancing together. She slipped her robe completely off and pulled at his shirt.

"I need skin. Take this off."

He deposited her on the bed with a suck to her nipple and a swipe on her pulsing pussy. "Give me a second, honey."

Adelaide listened to him undress, anxious to see what was hidden in the gloom of the night. The thump of his boots, the rasp of his trousers as they traveled down his skin, the slight sound of his shirt fluttering to land on the floor. Within moments, he was on top of her, hard and rough.

It seemed as if her entire body sighed in relief. As he slid into her welcoming warmth, this time the pace was less frantic, less urgent. Adelaide savored Trevor, the feel of him within her, on her, all around her. The sweet, slow love brought her a place she'd never been.

As they snuggled together, exhausted, she fell asleep wondering how to stay away from him now that he was in her blood.

ꕥ

Buster watched through the window until the couple walked upstairs. His hand steadily caressed his hardened staff. Even if she was a bitch, she had tits that made his mouth water, and he'd love to get his hands on that cunt. He quickly finished himself off, leaving his seed on the wall outside her building. Served her right for trying to take over business he'd spent ten years building. After only two years of living and working, she'd thought she could take his town away from him.

Not a chance. Adelaide Burns would pay for it. The man he'd hired to shoot her dead had failed miserably, then the coward skipped town.

So the bitch spread her thighs for the handsome cowboy? That told McGee the fool meant something to her. Since Buster had been watching her, she hadn't taken any men to her bed.

He could use the drifter to force Adelaide to sell to him. One way or another. With a grin, he buttoned up his trousers and headed back to the Silver Spittoon to make plans.

Chapter Eight

The morning sun streamed through the curtains, making the room too bright. Trevor fought against the light, tunneling underneath the pillow. His arm brushed against a warm softness that wasn't supposed to be in his bed. Without opening his eyes, he knew it was female.

Hell, his bed didn't have soft sheets either, much less a woman.

He breathed in her scent. Adelaide. The memory of the night before rushed through him and his dick awoke with a yowl, hungry for more. His mouth remembered her lips, her breasts, the tang of her skin.

Unable to stay still any longer, he lightly caressed her arm, feeling the small hairs stand up under his fingers. The goose bumps ran faster than he did. She shifted her arm away and suddenly there was a whole lot of air under the covers. She'd gotten out of bed.

Damn.

"Time to get moving, Malloy." She sounded distracted and annoyed. What did she have to be annoyed about? It was she who started the encounters the night before.

Before Trevor could even answer her, the door closed with a snick and he was alone. He'd hoped for some early morning loving, not a dismissal. A rude dismissal at that. Not exactly what he was used to either. Seemingly against his will, he rolled over on his side and picked up her pillow. As he pressed it to his face, he inhaled deeply, and his hand crept down to his burgeoning cock and stroked. A shiver raced up his skin as he imagined Adelaide's hand instead of his own.

"Get out of my bed, there's work to be done."

Thwack!

Shock replaced arousal. He hadn't even heard her come back in the bedroom. He'd been somewhat caught up in his imaginings...and his hand. Trevor could not believe she actually spanked him on the ass. He was so shocked he completely forgot he was naked and hopped out of bed, ready to give Adelaide a piece of his mind.

Dustin stood at the door, a sardonic grin on his face, with Adelaide nowhere in sight.

There Trevor was, naked as a jaybird. With a hard-on. Son of a bitch.

"Time to work, pretty boy. Find a pair of pants to cover that up before you put an eye out." Dustin chuckled as he turned to leave.

"Funny, big boy."

"I thought so. Hurry up." Dustin's wide shoulders disappeared from view.

Trevor cursed and started searching for his clothes.

ꙮ

A month into working off his marker, Trevor stared at the shovel in Dustin's hand. He couldn't have heard that right.

"You want me to do what?"

"You need to clean the potatoes out of your ears? Dig a new hole for the outhouse." Dustin pointed to a spot marked with a stake about fifteen feet from the original outhouse. "Right there."

"Why on Sunday? Don't you all go to church or anything?" Trevor groused.

Dustin laughed and pushed the shovel into Trevor's hands. "Oh, sure, they welcome saloon owners and ex-convicts all the time."

"You're an ex-convict? What were you in for?" Trevor asked before he could stop his wayward tongue.

"None of your fucking business. Now take the shovel. We need a new hole and you're digging it."

Chasing strays and counting cows sounded pretty good at the moment. Why the hell had he ever left Cheshire? Trevor took the shovel with a snatch that earned him a splinter. When the hell had he gotten to be such a whiny ass baby?

After he'd met Adelaide Burns and discovered life wasn't always going to go his way. He was smart enough to realize that. Didn't mean he had to accept it and start acting like an adult. He wasn't done being angry about it.

He stared at the hard, scrubby ground with a sneer. As if that would change what he had to do. Dammit to hell.

Two hours later, Trevor's back screamed and his hands were covered with blisters. He'd finished the four foot hole. Now he just had to move the current outhouse on top of the new hole, and fill in the old one. The stench from it was enough to make him gag.

Not a task he looked forward to.

"Did you stop working already?" Dustin was beginning to sound like a nagging wife.

"I finished this hole. Now I need some help moving that building"—he pointed to the outhouse—"over this hole. You think you can do that?"

Dustin's eyes narrowed. "I might be big, but I ain't a fool, cowboy. You'll be sorry if you forget that."

Trevor threw up his hands. "Fine. I'll be nice, I promise. Can you help me now?"

"What will you give me?" Dustin asked.

"My undying love."

The big man burst out laughing and Trevor felt a grin tug his lips. "Or maybe I promise not to kick your ass today."

Fresh guffaws rocked him so Trevor figured Dustin wasn't going to be much help at all. He opened the outhouse door and a few flies buzzed into his face. Waving his hand, he took the paper for visitors—obviously not using the Sears & Roebuck catalog for ordering purposes—and threw it to the side.

"Did you die in here, Dustin? Whew, it sure does stink."

The walls were stained darker in some places, lighter in others. Apparently the patrons of the Last Chance Saloon weren't able to aim with regularity. There wasn't even a seat around the hole to prevent splinters on your ass, or in worse places. The seat was something his pa always had installed in the outhouse before he put in the indoor privy. Trevor never guessed he had it so good. The wood around the hole was worn and uneven. He reminded himself that his ass had sat there on more than one occasion.

Still laughing, Dustin slapped him on the back hard enough to send him into the outhouse. He stopped himself from falling too far, thank God. Sure as shooting, he didn't need to smell like shit in addition to feeling like it. Fortunately or not, he got a few more splinters—kept his mind off the pain from the blisters anyway.

The building shifted beneath him and he grabbed the edges of the door to steady himself.

"Just a minute!" he shouted. "Let me get a grip on this side."

He planted his hands under the building and readied himself. "One, two, three!"

It seemed he hadn't underestimated Dustin's strength. Trevor hardly strained at all, he simply shifted it to the right fifteen feet to the new hole. With a set of grunts, they placed the building right over its new home.

Before Trevor could say anything, Dustin disappeared back into the saloon. For being such a big tough guy, he'd surprised Trevor by actually helping. Without Dustin, it probably would have taken two hours to move that building by himself.

Damn. He didn't want to feel indebted to anyone else. Jesus please us.

He glanced at the pile of dirt and the hated shovel, then at the nasty, stinking hole he needed to fill in. As his mother said, sooner started, sooner finished. Too bad it smelled bad enough to steal his appetite for a week.

Trevor pulled off his shirt, wiped his forehead with it and got back to work, secretly plotting to give Adelaide a nice, tight hug when he was done.

Adelaide couldn't help herself. She wandered toward the kitchen for coffee and found herself by the window. If she were honest with herself, she did try not to look, but not too hard. Trevor talked to himself as he dug. The man definitely knew how to put in a good day's work. Shovelfuls of dirt flew through the air at a remarkable pace. It should have surprised her, but it didn't. Even if he was a charming gambler, a flirt and a ladies man, he seemed the type to help when prompted. Or ordered.

"You watching that cowboy, Miss Adelaide?" Marybeth asked from behind her.

"No, just looking at the birds," Adelaide lied through her teeth.

Marybeth snorted and punched the bread dough she was kneading on the butcher block table.

"He is a nice-looking man," Adelaide offered lamely.

"That he is and quite a charmer too. I hear he charmed his way into your bed."

Bam, bam. Marybeth pounded harder.

"And you don't think that's a good idea?" Adelaide didn't think it was a good idea either, but she couldn't seem to help herself. Trevor was like a decadent dessert, rich and sweet, sinfully indulgent. In fact, she salivated for another taste.

Marybeth touched her arm. Adelaide turned to look into her friend's concerned eyes. "You be careful, Adelaide. I'm sure he's broken more than a few hearts in his life."

It constantly surprised Adelaide that folks like Marybeth and Dustin cared about her. They went out of their way to protect her, befriend her, and be there when she needed them. From a life of only looking out for herself, it took a long time to accept friends. Even longer to offer the same in return.

"Don't worry. I'm just...scratching an itch." Adelaide shrugged.

"Hopefully you won't get a rash from it."

Adelaide nearly spit coffee all over the window laughing. "Marybeth! I never know what to expect from you."

Marybeth waved her hand in the air. "I just say what's on my mind. Just listen to me and keep your heart guarded. He'll break it if you let him."

With those words of wisdom, Marybeth went back to the bread dough, leaving Adelaide to digest the advice. Was Marybeth right? Was she allowing Trevor to get too close? Physically, that wasn't a problem—they both enjoyed each other and that was that. No more, no less.

As far as her heart goes, she hadn't used it in quite a while. Probably didn't need to guard something that didn't work right.

Adelaide kept herself away from the kitchen for the next couple of hours. She balanced the books as she always did on Sundays, then straightened her desk. Her stomach reminded her it was nearly noon when it growled noisily.

Perhaps Trevor would be done and she wouldn't have to see him. Would it matter? More than likely. After the sex they'd had over the last month, touching him had become an addiction. She craved his scent, his cock, his hands. Trevor was a maestro of lovers and her body an instrument wanting to be played.

As Adelaide walked toward the kitchen for lunch, she wondered if perhaps Marybeth had a grain of truth in what she said. Adelaide's heart might not be at risk, but her peace of mind was. Dammit all, somehow she'd gotten herself involved with a man, regardless of her intentions not to.

She opened the door in time to see Dustin coming back inside laughing. His wide face didn't normally look so entertained, so she knew it had to do with Trevor.

"What did you do to him?" she asked with one eyebrow raised.

He pressed a hand to his chest. "Me? I helped that pretty boy move the outhouse. He was too little to do it himself." That sent Dustin off into a guffaw of laughter that made him clutch his stomach.

Adelaide shook her head and pushed past Dustin. "You can be such an ass sometimes."

Wrenching open the back door, Adelaide prepared herself to find Trevor in trouble. She didn't expect to find him shirtless, shoveling dirt into the old outhouse hole. She also didn't expect to have the sight of him half-naked, sweaty and covered with dirt to kick her like a gun recoil.

Holy Mary.

Trevor always joined her in the darkness or semi-darkness. She'd never seen him in broad daylight without his clothes. Her body tightened in arousal as his muscles bunched and moved like a symphony of man. Little rivers of sweat snaked their way down his back into the waistband of his trousers. Her nipples puckered and her hands clenched, wanting, *no*, needing to touch him. To be touched by him. To lick and explore all that magnificent bronzed flesh.

Adelaide stepped outside, unable to stop herself from reaching for him. Until the shovel almost whacked her on the head. It was as if someone threw a bucket of ice water on her. She'd been in a trance and probably would have grabbed him like a hussy if the shovel hadn't intervened. Or rather, if he hadn't brought the shovel back far enough to nearly hit her.

Walking on her toes, she slipped back into the house. Thank God he hadn't seen her.

Marybeth frowned and shook her finger. Adelaide frowned back, snatched an apple from the table and stomped out of the kitchen. Her appetite had vanished and been replaced by confused arousal.

ຣ໑ଔ

Trevor tossed the shovel toward the back of the saloon with a self-satisfied grunt. Finally. He was sure as hell damn well done with it. Thank God. His stomach was touching his backbone and a big fat lunch sounded perfect. Of course, he thought sourly, Marybeth would make him wash. Better finish up so he could get a sandwich and a beer.

He stepped all over the hole he'd just filled in to make sure the dirt was packed down tightly. At least the smell was better with the dirt over it. However, his nose hadn't recovered yet. No wonder Adelaide didn't want her patrons pissing in her private privy. God knows what it would look like after they got through with it.

Sweat poured down his body, pooling in the waistband of his trousers and making him itch. What he really needed was a bath, a nice cool one in clean water. Preferably with soap. He picked up his shirt and wiped his face with it, then swiped under his arms. It had to go in the wash anyway, might as well make use of it.

When he turned around, the smell of shit dissipated and he thought he caught a whiff of Adelaide's unique scent. Probably making sure he was working—he owed her a nice sweaty hug. Grinning, he headed toward the building and stepped inside.

"Oh, no you don't, Mr. Dirt. Take your filthy self back outside," Marybeth ordered the second his feet hit the floor.

"Give me two minutes, Marybeth. I need to give Miss Adelaide something." Despite the squawking, Trevor kept on walking, intent on reaching her. She who sent him out to dig a shithouse hole on a Sunday morning.

He saw Adelaide's back as she disappeared into her office. Trevor broke into a run and caught up to her in seconds. She gasped as he grabbed her arm and pulled her flush against his sweaty, filthy body.

"Good afternoon, Red. I thought I'd show you what you're paying for." He shifted up and down and back and forth, really rubbing his salty wetness into her nice clean clothes.

"Get off me, Malloy! Ugh, you are disgusting. And that smell? Is that just you or the new privy?" She pushed at him, but he didn't let loose. He was enjoying feeling her squirm, and making her pay for sending him to the shitter.

"Am I dirty, lover?" He licked her earlobe, then sucked it with a nibble to boot.

"Beyond dirty. Now let me go before I get sick all over you." She inhaled sharply when he blew in the delicate pink shell of her ear.

"Are you sure you want me to let go?" he whispered.

"Yesssss. I mean...you need a bath." She inhaled then coughed. "Really, really need a bath."

"Are you going to give me one?" The very thought of Adelaide washing him was enough to make him rock hard. Her long-fingered hands soaping him up, washing every nook and cranny, touching, caressing. The more he imagined, the more he decided it was an excellent idea.

"Me give you a bath? What do you think this is, a whorehouse?" Her words implied an insult, but her tone said otherwise.

"Mmmm, no, but it is a woman's house." He nuzzled her neck and sucked at the skin near her collarbone. "Please, honey."

"I s-suppose...it will definitely make you cleaner. The stench is making my eyes water."

Trevor's hand crept down to cup her mound. "Your eyes are not the only thing that's wet. So hot, so ready."

She moaned and dug her nails into his shoulders. And damn, she had sharp nails. Nearly broke the skin.

"Let's go upstairs." Adelaide liked to order. She pushed against his shoulder and he let her free. After she walked away from him, Trevor stood for a moment catching his breath. She turned and looked at him, her eyes intense, and cocked one eyebrow.

Shaking his head, Trevor followed like the obedient puppy he was. Holy hell, how did she get him so wrapped around her finger? She told him he stunk and he got a hard-on. Who knew he had such a weakness for bossy women?

Adelaide was embarrassed by the state of her knickers. After watching him half-naked like a giggling schoolgirl, she transformed into a puddle of flesh when he pressed against her. Even though he was dirty, sweaty and stinky, she couldn't seem to stop herself from wanting him. Badly.

Somehow they made it to her private bathing room without anyone seeing them. He shut the door and twisted the key with a snick. When he saw the enormous clawfooted tub, his eyes widened, and then his smile did.

"My, my, Miss Adelaide. You've been keeping secrets. How did you get a tub that big? And I'm sure there's indoor hot water. You like the best, right?" He walked toward her slowly, like a predator stalking her, unbuttoning his trousers as he went. A shiver danced up her spine when she realized she liked it. Being hunted was never one of her priorities before. Before Trevor that is.

Her nipples popped and his gaze strayed to the pert points under her dress. When he licked his lips, Adelaide almost ripped his pants off herself.

"Start the water, honey," Trevor said as he reached for the waistband of his trousers and started pushing them down.

Adelaide whirled around and fumbled with the tub until the water rushed out. She closed her eyes and tried to center herself. No need turning into a blithering idiot.

Trevor's hands landed on her shoulders and she sucked in a breath of surprise. His hardened cock pressed against her back. Moisture flooded her pussy as it recalled just how talented that tool was.

"You've got too many clothes on." He reached around to unbutton her dress, which fortunately only had a dozen buttons down the front. When it gaped open, he cupped her breasts and his thumbs teased her distended nipples. She leaned against him and felt the pleasure trickle down from his touch.

In moments, her dress was in a puddle around her feet and her chemise thrown in the corner. Still he stood behind her, caressing her with his callused hands. He nudged her legs apart so two fingers could dip into her wetness and rub her clit in slow, maddening circles. His tongue lapped at her ears and neck, sucking and nibbling as he went.

The other hand worked its magic on her nipple, bringing it to a peak that begged to be bitten, yet he stayed behind her. Steam from the water swirled around them, heating Adelaide's body even further. She felt lost in a haze of arousal and pleasure, a spell woven by a master seducer.

And she loved it.

God help her, it was addicting and amazing. She spread her legs further and soon he was fucking her with his fingers while the heel of his hand continued to tease her clit. When Trevor pinched her nipple at the same time another finger teased her ass, Adelaide came so hard and so fast, she literally saw stars behind her eyes. She bucked against him, moaning his name and feeling his cock nestle against her, humping her even as she humped him.

Adelaide tried to take a deep breath, but the steam and the intensity of the orgasm that had just overtaken her made it difficult. Before she could protest, Trevor swooped her up into his arms and stepped into the tub. After he nestled her against him in the depths of the hot bath, he turned off the water.

Floating. That's what it felt like. Floating on a sea with a pirate of pleasure. She giggled at her own foolish thoughts.

"What's so funny?"

She shook her head. "Nothing. Just my own schoolgirl fantasies."

"Fantasies? Any of them involve me?" Trevor continued to caress her, relax her, as her body came down from its incredible high. Another thing in his favor, he was so completely aware of her needs and never forgot them.

His needs were poking her in the backside. He hadn't achieved a release, obviously, so it was time Adelaide took that situation in her hands.

Literally.

She sat up and turned around so she was on her knees. He looked amazing—covered in a sheen of steam and sweat, with rivulets of water running down his bronzed chest. It seemed to surprise her every day that a man who looked as good as he would choose to pursue a thirty-year-old saloon owner with a bad attitude. She couldn't explain why, but knew she'd enjoy it as long as she could.

"My turn."

At her announcement, he raised one eyebrow and grinned. "I can't wait."

Adelaide reached for the French-milled soap she always used. She lathered up her hands, then knelt between his legs. Her palms actually itched to touch him, wash him, caress him. It was difficult to ignore the cock that was inches from her.

She started with his face and neck, which she rinsed immediately, making sure no soap got in his eyes. Next, she soaped his hair, mindful of the tender spot from her spittoon whack weeks earlier. He had gloriously thick hair that sometimes reminded her of the sunset with its hues of brown, gold and red. As she scratched his scalp, he moaned and squeezed her waist.

"Ah, God, honey, that feels so good."

His husky tone sent arrows of need through her and she had a hard time concentrating on not fucking him senseless yet. God knows it was hard to keep her legs closed.

"Scoot forward so I can rinse your hair."

As Adelaide moved back, he slid forward, which brought his mouth up next to her breasts. Adelaide took the cup from the shelf beside the tub and rinsed his hair. Apparently the temptation grew too big because he started licking her nipple, then it was in his mouth and he sucked deeply. His hand pinched and teased the other nipple. Back and forth he went, making Adelaide's concentration falter.

"Trevor. I...you're making it hard to bathe you."

"Mmmm...but you taste so good, sweet Red. I had to lick you, bite you"—he bit her nipple hard enough to make her jerk—"and make you feel good. I can't help myself."

After finishing his hair, she let him continue a few moments longer until her breaking point grew too close. Then she pulled away. He tried to yank her back, but she smacked his head.

"No. It's time to stop. For now."

Looking like a pouting school boy, he let her go and slid back into the tub.

Adelaide took a shaky breath while her body pulsed and pounded with need. "Now let's finish washing you."

She soaped up her hands again and washed his shoulders, arms, chest and back, reveling in the feel of the muscles and skin beneath her fingers. He had a few scars here and there, as most men do. Trevor felt like a bowstring, taut and ready, yet he never rushed her or complained that she spent too much time. Adelaide rinsed his top half, then prepared herself for the next part.

"Stand up so I can wash...the rest of you."

Trevor did as she bade, the water rushing off him as he stood in the tub with her kneeling before him. His erection jutted proudly, announcing itself to the world. Adelaide wanted to put her mouth on him, but she concentrated on getting him clean first.

A fresh handful of soap and the sweet torture began. By the time she had finished his ass, Trevor had moaned twice. When she washed his legs, he quivered beneath her touch. Saving the best for last, she fondled, cleaned and caressed Trevor's balls until they were as tight as walnuts.

Adelaide circled his cock with her soapy hands and slowly ran up and down the shaft. She tickled, teased and tortured him until the veins were nearly as hard as he was.

"Be careful, honey. That gun's ready to fire," he choked out as he trembled against her.

When her hands released him, he grabbed the wall, she assumed to keep himself upright. With a secret grin, she rinsed him off, taking some extra time to be sure there was no soap left in the nest of hair surrounding his beautiful hard-on.

After the last cup of water splashed over him, Adelaide took him in her mouth and used her tongue and lips to slide down his hardness. He groaned and grasped her shoulders.

Yes.

He tasted like man, like Trevor, like the sweetest ambrosia. She ran her tongue around the head, lapping like a kitten with cream. Then she took him deep, as deep as she could, feeling him tap the back of her throat. Then back up to the head, then down to the base. Not a steady rhythm, but one to drive him mad. While her mouth tantalized him, she cupped his balls and squeezed lightly. Already the salty taste of his seed coated her tongue. He wouldn't last long.

The question was, did she want him to find his release yet?

He took that decision out of her hands when he stepped back and hauled her up against him. His eyes were wide, the pupils dilated, and his nostrils flared. Gone was the sweet, teasing man who constantly smiled and flirted with her. This man wanted to mate, to fuck, to plunge into her and howl.

With a strength she didn't know he had, he picked her up and wrapped her legs around his back. He entered her quickly with a hard thrust that made her entire body clench. Full, complete, stretched, so good.

"Ah, God... Red, I can't..." With those mumbled words, he stepped out of the tub, still nestled deep within her. Holding her with one arm, he threw a towel on the floor with his free hand, then laid her down quickly. She spread her legs and felt him go so deep, he touched her womb.

"Now, Trevor."

It was the fiercest mating they'd had. Like two beasts snarling, clawing and slamming into each other, frenzied with desire and need. She held onto him with her fingernails while he pumped into her again and again. Trevor bit her nipples while she bit his shoulders. Teeth and tongues clashed as their mouths fused as one.

Within minutes, they both reached their peak, shouting together, thrusting harder. Once. Twice. Three times.

“Adelaide!”

“Trevor!”

It wasn’t God they called out to as they found a place that they’d only reached as one. A place they’d never been to before with anyone else. They called to each other. Adelaide knew then that she’d lied to Marybeth.

Sure as shooting, her heart was most definitely involved.

Chapter Nine

Buster McGee paced on the worn wooden floor in the backroom of the Silver Spittoon. His boots thunked like a heartbeat as he made his rounds back and forth. That goddamned bitch was making his life hell.

Nothing he'd done had worked and he had run out of options. It was time to do something more permanent.

Time to hire someone who knew what he was doing.

ᘓᘕ

After Kincaid stepped inside, it took about fifteen seconds to get a bead on every gun in the Last Chance Saloon, including the shotgun under the bar. That one was currently being handled by a huge bartender with a pair of eyebrows that resembled a small animal. He'd spotted Kincaid immediately—a kindred spirit.

He marked the redheaded lady dealer at one of the tables in the back. She wore a velvet green getup while she dealt cards with a smile and a wickedly fast pair of hands. Kincaid pushed back his hat and sauntered to the bar, nodding to the giant.

"Evenin'," he offered without a smile, but friendly enough in tone.

"Evenin'. What'll you have?" The giant's voice matched the size of his fists. Deep and dark.

"Beer." Kincaid put four bits on the bar and waited for his drink.

The man sweeping the floor on the far side of the saloon watched Kincaid carefully. He was a mite too big, too clean and too lethal to be doing that. In fact, he looked as if he needed a pair of guns strapped to his legs to be complete. Definitely one to keep an eye on.

The bartender slammed down the beer in front of Kincaid, yet he didn't flinch. Instead, he nodded his thanks and picked it up.

"You passing through?" the bartender growled.

"No, I'm in town looking for work. Round-up is going on right about now, right?" Kincaid tried to sound dumb.

"Round-up is over for ranches hereabouts. Don't think anyone is hiring."

Well, it was obvious that the man had no compunction about telling Kincaid there was no place for him. He wasn't worried—in fact, he expected it. Counted on it.

"Well, I'll just hang around for a few days then. Maybe play some poker." Kincaid took out a few bills from his pocket and glanced up. "Can anyone join the game or do you need an invite?"

With a scowl, the bartender jerked his head toward the tables. His gaze clearly told Kincaid that he'd be watched. Closely.

After he picked up his beer, Kincaid walked toward the redhead's game, controlling his breathing and giving the appearance of a regular cowboy. The man sweeping the floor kept an eye on Kincaid as he walked. By the time he reached the game, the other man was behind the redhead, glaring at him with the protective air of a lover.

So that's the way of things. That little piece of information would come in mighty handy.

"Evenin', ma'am. Can I join in the game?"

She looked him over and motioned to the empty chair. "Dollar ante, stranger."

Kincaid sat, keeping his gaze from the cowboy with the intense stare.

Adelaide could not shake the feeling that the stranger was dangerous. Perhaps it was his nearly colorless eyes, or the fact that he walked like a big cat. She believed in her instincts, counted on them to keep her safe in a world populated by men.

"Ante up, fellas. Five card draw, threes are wild."

The stranger's hands were covered with calluses, but relatively clean. He held his cards like a man used to sitting at a poker table. She could feel Trevor behind her in the shadows. A comforting presence. He stayed there, as if he sensed her unease, or perhaps he was uneasy too.

"Can I get your name, lady dealer?"

She hesitated, but felt the other players looking at her strangely. Adelaide was as tough as they come; she shouldn't be cowed by a stranger sitting at her table.

"You may call me Miss Adelaide."

"Kincaid."

The name echoed through her brain. Familiar, yet not. She couldn't quite put her finger on *who* he was, but she had a feeling she knew *what* he was.

The stranger won the first game, a modest pot. Then he proceeded to win the second and third hands as well, each time putting a bit more in his pocket. Adelaide watched him closely, trying to catch him cheating. To her consternation, she couldn't see anything out of the ordinary. The man knew how to play poker really, really well.

Too well.

It was almost as if he was throwing down a gauntlet from gambler to gambler. Testing her or taunting her. It was working, too. Adelaide played harder, using her skills to win a hand. The stranger nodded when he saw her straight.

"Very nice, Miss Adelaide. I see I have some real competition," Kincaid said, but his gaze was on Trevor.

The hackles on the back of Adelaide's neck rose. She felt a tingling in her hands and feet. Trevor's anger grew palpable—she could almost see it in the air. Something was going to happen if she didn't stop it.

Adelaide stood abruptly, cutting off the staring contest between Trevor and Kincaid. "Sorry, gentlemen, but it's time for a dealer change."

She signaled to Jason to come over and he was there in moments. "This is Jason, he'll be your dealer for the rest of the evening." With a nod to each player, Adelaide turned. Trevor stared at her with fierceness in his gaze. He held out his arm and she took it like a real lady. Together they walked toward the bar and Dustin. Adelaide knew Kincaid was looking at her, nearly boring holes in her back. A shiver danced down her spine.

Trevor's hand covered hers and he squeezed. Adelaide watched Dustin and leaned on Trevor, feeling as safe as she could be with two protectors.

Dustin's scowl could frighten children and small animals. "I like that stranger less than pretty boy here." He jerked his thumb toward Trevor.

"I don't like him either," Adelaide admitted.

Trevor growled, "I want to toss him out on his ass. Then beat the shit out of him."

Dustin's eyebrows shot up. "You surprise me, Malloy. I figured you to be a pussy."

"I think you just insulted me, you son of a bitch." Trevor's scowl grew blacker.

Adelaide moved between them again. "Relax, Trevor. The stranger didn't do anything but play a few hands of poker."

"He cleaned out three men's pockets and played like a professional. Don't tell me he did nothing." Trevor's grip tightened. "That man is dangerous."

"I agree. Kincaid gave me the willies."

"What did you say his name was?" Dustin's gaze moved to the back of the saloon, to the stranger who had put a knot in all their tails.

"He said it was Kincaid. Mean anything to you?" Trevor stepped closer to the bar.

Dustin nodded. "I know that name. He's a hired gun."

Adelaide's stomach cramped. Would Buster go so far as to hire someone to kill her? "Are you sure it's the same man?"

Trevor turned her until she faced him. He cupped her face and looked at her with anger, concern and a smattering of real fear. Now she knew she wasn't imagining things. Her battle to keep her saloon open just took a nasty turn, as if the potshot at her weeks ago wasn't nasty.

"I'm sure. As soon as Dustin said it, I was sure and so were you. Let's not take a chance." He looked at the bigger man. "Ready to take out the trash, big man?"

Dustin broke into a wide grin and cracked his knuckles. "Oh, yeah, let's go, pretty boy."

Trevor shook his finger at Adelaide. "Go upstairs to your room and lock the door."

"No. I'm not leaving my saloon, no matter who that man is." Adelaide wasn't about to give over everything she'd worked for.

Trevor ran his hands down his face and looked as frustrated as she felt. "Look, Red, I don't want you to be in any danger. I can't protect you if you don't protect yourself."

"Malloy, I don't need a knight in shining armor. I need a friend."

Although he appeared ready to throw her over his shoulders, he simply stared at her. "You're a stubborn, cussed woman."

"Thank you."

"It wasn't meant as a compliment, Red."

"Yep, but it was. Now are we going to get rid of that shyster, or not?" She quirked one eyebrow and waited for Dustin and Trevor to accept the fact that she would never run from a battle, no matter what the odds or the outcome.

"Fine." Trevor's tone told her it was anything but. "At least let me stand between you and that cannon on his hip."

Adelaide rolled her eyes and sighed. "If it will make you feel better."

"God, you are going to unman me." With a scowl that resembled Dustin's, Trevor looked back at the table at which Kincaid sat.

Dustin touched her elbow lightly. "He's trying to help, Adelaide."

Trevor nodded, glancing at the bigger man with surprise.

"Are you his friend now? Defending him?" Adelaide felt a pinch of jealousy.

"No, well, maybe. I dunno, but I do know that he's worried about you and so am I. That Kincaid is a cold-blooded killer and if he's after you, then you should be worried too." Dustin's eyes reflected the depth of his concern and Adelaide's heart thumped because of her friend.

"Thank you, Dustin." She cupped his big cheek. "We'll stand together and win together."

"Let Malloy stand with us."

"Listen to Dustin, Red. He's making good sense."

She wanted to roll her eyes at Trevor suddenly agreeing with Dustin, instead she ignored him. She hadn't expected Dustin to form a bond with Trevor, but there it was, plain as day. That told her Malloy was more than the gambling ladies man he projected to the rest of the world. Dustin had razor-sharp instincts and he trusted them. Adelaide wasn't as certain about Trevor, but she'd try. For Dustin's sake.

Ignoring the little demon jumping on her shoulder and calling her a liar, Adelaide nodded at Dustin.

"Okay, we'll trust Malloy. For now." She raised one eyebrow in Trevor's direction, to which he responded with a small lip twitch.

Dustin turned to Trevor. "Let's take out the trash."

Trevor's grin was as wicked and cold as she'd ever seen. "Gladly."

They approached the table from either side, with Adelaide walking behind Trevor. Kincaid was on his feet facing them before they got within ten feet of the table. His stance was casual, but his hand rested near his pistol.

"There a problem, folks?" Kincaid asked.

"I reckon it's time for you to mosey on home, stranger," Trevor said with a tight smile. "Saloon is closing."

"Closing, eh? Do they know that?" Kincaid looked around at the dozens of people drinking, playing poker and watching the action closely.

"Of course they do," Adelaide interjected over Trevor's shoulder. "They're all my regulars. It's time for you to move on, mister."

Trevor immediately stepped in front of her view. She wanted to kick him in the ass for it.

"Move along," Dustin growled. "Tonight's over for you."

Kincaid held up his hands. "No problem. I'm leaving. Figure I'll go get me some grub at that restaurant down the street." He tipped his hat to Adelaide. "Thank you for the poker game, Miss Adelaide."

It seemed that the world held its breath as Kincaid strolled slowly out of the Last Chance Saloon. His boots scraped softly on the wood floor and Adelaide swore she heard her own heart beating it was so quiet.

ꞮꞮ

Brett Malloy cursed his brother Trevor for the thousandth time on a rainy morning over a month after he'd left. Every goddamn day, he had to muck the stalls by himself, taking twice as long, then of course he was late for the rest of the days' chores. Pa refused to allow any of the other hands to help so that left Brett out of luck and annoyed. More like angry.

"Need a hand?"

Brett looked up to find his nephew Noah standing at the stall entrance.

"What are you doing here?"

Noah shrugged. “Ma wanted to visit for a few days so I drew wagon duty.”

“Nicky’s always been like that. Doing stuff on a whim whenever she felt like it.” Brett loved his sister, but she could be as big a pain in the ass as Trevor. Damn his sorry hide.

Noah picked up a pitchfork and together they worked quietly. Brett wasn’t one to speak just to pass the time like his siblings. He spoke when he had something to say. Some folks considered him standoffish or odd because of it, but Brett couldn’t change who he was for anyone.

“You hear from Trevor?” Noah asked as he brought the wheelbarrow back in full of fresh straw.

Brett clenched his jaw to keep from barking an answer. It wasn’t Noah’s fault that every blessed person on the planet asked him that same damned question every damned day.

“No.”

“I’m worried about him. It’s not like Uncle Trevor to not send word for so long.” Noah echoed Brett’s sentiments exactly. He was worried, but he’d be double-dipped if he’d admit it.

“He probably found some saloon girl and professed his undying love to her. I’m sure he’ll be home when his money runs out.” Brett started forking the hay in the stall with a vengeance.

“Still, don’t you think we ought to go after him?”

Brett gazed at Noah and saw that somewhere along the way the little orphan boy had become a man. Probably weeks away from twenty-one, the young man had filled out to have broad shoulders and chest, a deep voice, and a stubborn, persistent nature akin to both his adopted parents.

“I wasn’t planning on it. Are you?” Brett asked the question in jest, but the look in Noah’s eyes told him that he wasn’t kidding. Noah planned on following Trevor. "When were you planning on leaving?"

"Today or tomorrow. When I told Ma, she laughed and told me I was a good Malloy." Noah made a face. "Pa doesn't know yet."

Brett's eyebrows climbed toward his hairline. "Are you telling me that you planned on sneaking off without telling your pa, who happens to be your boss, that you were leaving?"

Noah's cheeks turned slightly pink. "I told Ma."

"Hmph. Fat lot of good that will do you when Tyler catches up with your scrawny ass. That ex-bounty hunter will track you, you know. He wasn't always a rancher and a father." Brett knew all too well how hard his brother-in-law could be. Damn good thing he fell in love with Brett's sister, Nicky, before he could turn her in for the bounty she'd had on her head.

"I'm counting on it." Noah's brave words were accompanied by a slight tremor.

Brett had a lot of respect for his nephew and it just went up even higher. Noah was worried enough about Trevor to risk his father's wrath, and trick Tyler into helping to find Trevor. He was not only clever and dangerous, but foolhardy and a true Malloy.

"Your ma is right, Noah, you are a Malloy." Brett clapped his nephew on the shoulder, surprised to discover they stood eye to eye. Yep, Noah was ready to be a man.

"Let's finish up here and then go tell your grandma. She's been bothering me for two weeks to go after Trevor." Brett focused on forking the hay as quickly as he could. Suddenly the idea of chasing after his wayward brother had promise.

He couldn't wait to kick Trevor's ass when he found him.

ꟷ

In the great room of the Malloy house, Francesca stared at her grandson and son with a hard gaze. Brett felt a squirm working its way up from his feet and he fought against it. For God's sake, he wasn't a boy, he didn't need his mother's permission to leave home and find his brother.

"It's raining."

Brett sighed. "I know it's raining, Mama, but it's nearly mid-summer when things start drying up. Now is the time to go before the busy fall season starts."

His mother nodded and continued to stare him down. Brett refused to break his stare off first. He could stare with the best of them. Noah almost immediately looked away. Even if she was his grandmother, Francesca Malloy was a tough woman when she wanted to be and she could intimidate the most powerful men with the "evil glare" as his brother Jack called it.

"How long will you be gone?"

"Mama, look, we don't know how long we'll be gone. Let's say two weeks. If we haven't found him by then, we'll come home. Before you ask, we can't take the train because we know he didn't. We need to follow his path on a horse, toward Texas." Brett bracketed his hips with his hands. "I swear we will wire you every other day."

"You're darned right you will. I don't want another one of my son's disappearing or my oldest grandson either. Take plenty of food, and your slickers and dry clothes. Oh, and—"

Brett threw his hands in the air. "I can pack for a trail ride, Mama. Please just give us your blessing so we can go."

Francesca looked like she wanted to say more, but she kept her mouth shut and turned her gaze to Nicky. Nicky sat at the table holding her youngest child, baby Francesca or "Frankie" on her lap. His sister had the same look of concern in her eyes that Noah sported. Frankie had her father's dark hair and her mother's aim with a wooden spoon since she kept whacking it on the table.

"Mama, we need to find out where he is. I already contacted Malcolm down in Texas and you know Trevor never showed up there. I'm worried. Please let them go. Brett will look out for Noah." Nicky chewed at her lower lip. "You know I wouldn't let Noah go unless I knew he'd be okay."

Francesca frowned and looked between her children. "You have my blessing." She shook her finger in Brett's face. "If you miss one day with your telegram, I'm coming after you."

Brett couldn't help but grin at the fierceness in the five-foot-tall woman in front of him. He picked her up and gave her a tight squeeze until she squawked. "Thank you, Mama."

He met Noah's gaze and nodded. They could leave within the hour and God help Trevor if he was stopped in a saloon somewhere getting drunk and falling into bed with some woman.

Chapter Ten

Trevor could barely control the urge to follow that piece of shit Kincaid and make him leave town. Permanently. Without a weapon, not even a measly knife in his boot, Trevor felt helpless and useless. A feeling he was definitely not used to. Good thing Dustin had that shotgun under the bar to wave at the hired gun or he'd probably have laughed at them.

Then shot Adelaide dead.

The thought of Adelaide lying dead made his entire body tremble and go cold as a mountain stream. No way in hell he'd ever allow that to happen, but to know that son of a bitch McGee hired a gunman to kill her turned on Trevor's fury like nobody's business.

He'd been brought up to respect, protect and revere women. The thought that a man could contemplate hurting a woman like that made Trevor angry. To think it was Adelaide drove him crazy.

He attacked the dirty dishes in the kitchen with a frenzy that made Marybeth step back a pace and stare. He didn't care what she thought. What he needed to do was get into a knock-down, drag-out fight, unfortunately none of his brothers were around. And the last time he tangled with Dustin, he got his head cracked open.

That night, Adelaide did not come to him and Trevor lay in bed wondering what he'd done wrong, if she was scared or lonely. After midnight passed, he couldn't stand it anymore so he went to her.

She stood near the window in a white nightdress so sheer the moonlight lit the perfection of her curves. Her breasts looked beautiful in the shadows of the cotton, the dark vee of her legs inviting and mysterious. Her hair was unbound, washing down her back like a waterfall against the fabric.

"Adelaide?" He wasn't sure if she'd heard him enter the room. When she didn't answer, Trevor stepped toward her. "What's the matter, honey?"

She shook her head slowly. "McGee is a bastard. I wanted to go right over to the Silver Spittoon and put a bullet in his heart."

Trevor was glad to know she felt the same way, yet scared she'd actually do it. Adelaide didn't need to get her neck stretched because of another man's greed.

He cupped her shoulders and pulled her back against his chest. "Ah, Red, we'll keep the wolves at bay. Kincaid won't be able to get back in and McGee must realize we know what he's trying to do. How about we go talk to the sheriff?"

"That's not going to do me much good. The sheriff thinks I'm a whore."

That word was like a hammer in Trevor's heart. "Tomorrow I'm going to go kick that sorry sheriff's ass for that."

Adelaide chuckled. "No need. I've already told him he's a pompous windbag who doesn't deserve to wear a tin star."

"Still, I'd like to pound him some."

She turned around and wrapped her arms around his back, tucking her head under his chin. "It's nice that you'd like to defend me, but I've been doing it for myself for so long, I don't need or want help."

Trevor wondered about Adelaide's life. Where she'd come from and how she ended up a poker-playing saloon owner.

"Tell me about yourself."

"Why would you want to know about me?"

"Well, I'm just curious... I'd be happy to tell you anything you want to know about me." Trevor rubbed his hands on her back in soothing circles. He could feel the tension knotting her up.

"I grew up in Texas, Oklahoma and a bit in Missouri. My granddaddy raised me for the most part. He gambled and drank most days." She shrugged. "He was a good man, with a good heart, just weak. My daddy died when I was young and my mother I never knew. That's all there is to me."

Oh, there was more than that to Adelaide Burns, and Trevor had a million questions. He held them back by sheer force of will.

"I would still like to defend you now and again, if it's okay. Not that I'm any catch." Trevor wanted do something besides sweep her floors.

"So you'll be my selfless knight in shining armor?"

"I'm as far from a knight as you can get without being an outlaw. So don't worry about me riding up on a noble steed." He laughed. "My brothers would argue with you about me ever being selfless. In fact, their word is selfish."

Adelaide pulled back and looked him square in the eye. "I guess they know you best then?"

Trevor kissed her on the forehead. "They don't know me at all."

That night their loving was slow and sensual, as if savoring each second they had together. Adelaide let him stay in her bed until they got up together in the morning and made love again.

Trevor was kidding himself if he thought it was anything but making love. Somewhere along the way, he'd fallen in love with the intractable Adelaide Burns. He watched her brush her hair, wash up, then dress. The entire time he simply stared, unable to move from his spot on the bed. She finally turned to him with a frown.

"What are you doing, Trevor?"

He liked it when she called him Trevor—she only did it when she wasn't mad at him or in the throes of passion. He sighed deeply and pinched the bridge of his nose.

"Just tired I think."

"Get up, then. It's Monday and the day's a wastin'. I think there's a wagonload of liquor coming in that you and Dustin need to unload." She braided her hair quickly then tied it off with a leather strip. She pursed her lips at him. "Did you hear me? What is wrong with you?"

Trevor stood and crossed the room, unembarrassed by his nakedness. Particularly when her gaze strayed to his cock, which gently slapped against his thigh in rest. When he reached her, he cupped her face in his hands and kissed her with everything that was in his heart—releasing the loneliness that he hadn't known was there before. Why hadn't he realized what a lonely existence he'd been living? A life without a partner to share it with was half a life.

Suddenly, coming to Cheyenne had become a stepping stone thrown in his path for a reason. That reason stood in front of him, gently scented by rosewater and whose delicious lips were still puffy from the night's activities. When he finally released her, she stared at him like he'd lost his mind.

Before she could say anything else, Trevor grinned and kissed the end of her nose. "Good morning, honey."

Whistling, he retrieved his clothes and headed, still naked, back down the hallway to his room. Adelaide's laughter followed him.

ꟈꟈ

Trevor was finishing the morning dishes when Dustin opened the kitchen door and peered in. His bushy eyebrows were already in the standard scowl that seemed to be a permanent part of his face.

"Hey, Malloy, I'm off to get the crates from the freight depot. Meet me out back in ten minutes to unload the shipment." Then he was gone just as quickly as he'd appeared.

Trevor saluted the air where Dustin's shaggy head had been. "Aye, aye, Captain Fur."

Marybeth couldn't stifle the giggle fast enough. Trevor heard it and looked at her with a grin. She stood by the stove, cutting up potatoes and carrots for the noon meal of beef stew.

"I heard that."

She shrugged. "Oh, so what? He's a big bear of a man who needs to be taught a lesson now and then. He takes life far too seriously all the time. No fun."

Trevor had come to the same conclusion the second he'd met the big man. "Why don't you make him have some fun?"

This time, Marybeth laughed out loud. "Me? What could I do?"

Trevor finished wiping the plate he had in his hand, then untied the apron around his waist. "Well, you could start by doing something fun with him. Like a picnic? With a special chocolate cake perhaps? I know he loves your cake."

Wonder of wonders, Marybeth actually blushed. Trevor had to control the urge to gape at her. He had the sneaking feeling that his kitchen curmudgeon had feelings for the bartender curmudgeon. They were perfect for each other. Right then and there, Trevor decided, even if his life went to hell, he would help Marybeth and Dustin find happiness together. Hopefully without bodily injury to Trevor in the process.

"Malloy!" Dustin's shout echoed from outside making the rafters shake a bit.

"That man is louder than a stampede of longhorns." Trevor headed outside to help unload the crates to the sound of Marybeth chuckling.

He found Dustin jumping down from the wagon loaded with crates of liquor. Big crates. Heavy crates. Many, many crates.

Trevor supposed it was better than dirty dishes.

Dustin opened the basement doors with a bang and grabbed a crate off the back of the wagon. He grunted at Trevor on the way by. "Get moving, Malloy. Keep your eye out too. I saw that snake Kincaid yesterday."

Trevor had seen him too. On more than one occasion. Most times just standing across the street smoking and watching the Last Chance. Trevor figured Kincaid was waiting for Adelaide to leave on her own so he could put a bullet in her heart. There was no way Trevor would let that happen. The problem as a hired gunman, Kincaid didn't get paid until his job was done. That meant Adelaide was still in danger and Trevor wasn't sure what to do about it. He wished, for a moment, that his brothers were there to help.

For the next fifteen minutes, Trevor hauled crates of liquor off the wagon and down the ten stairs to the basement. Back-breaking labor that gave Trevor a multitude of aches and too many splinters to count. When he came back up the steps for the fifty-seventh—or was it fifty-eighth?—time, Dustin was scowling at the paper in his hand then at the wagon.

"What's the matter?" Trevor panted while he leaned his hands on his knees.

"The count is off. There should be six more crates of whiskey. I think that bastard Miller at the freight depot's been taking some for his own stash." Dustin jerked his head toward the wagon. "You keep unloading. I'll be back in five minutes."

Trevor nodded and waved his hand as Dustin stomped off toward the alley between the buildings. Time for a drink of water at least. Feeling just a smidge guilty, Trevor went to the rain barrel on the dock and dipped his hands in to get them clean. After rubbing them together, he shrugged and wiped them on the back of his pants. Probably the least dirty part of his clothing.

He cupped his hands and brought some sweet cool water to his mouth. As he sipped, a *whack* sounded behind him, followed by the noise of glass breaking. He turned to find two unknown men beating on the crates with wooden clubs. Likely hired by Kincaid or McGee to do mischief.

"Hey, what the hell are you doing?" Trevor tried to grab one man, but he swung his club around and slammed it into the back of Trevor's knees.

He landed hard onto the wooden dock and the stranger went back to destroying Adelaide's liquor. A surge of anger rushed through him and Trevor rose, ignoring the pain in his legs. He snatched the club out of the first man's hand and knocked him upside the head with it. The bastard toppled like a felled tree.

The other son of a bitch was bigger, built a lot like Dustin. He stood on top of the last ten crates, smashing them for all he was worth and grinning at Trevor like the town's idiot.

"Get down offa there!" Trevor snarled. "I'll stick that club down your throat!"

The big man laughed and continued beating at the crates. Trevor leapt onto the wagon and swung his club at the stranger. He made contact with one massive shoulder, but bounced off and landed hard on some broken glass and whiskey. He was certain some of it got through his jacket and into his skin.

Trevor jumped back up in time to hear the hiss of a match. The big stranger grinned at him with yellowed teeth.

"Let's see if you can take the heat, cowboy."

With a flick of his wrist, he threw the match into spilled liquor at Trevor's feet then vaulted off the wagon. Flames whooshed up all around him and Trevor stumbled backwards onto the dock. Pain lanced through his legs as he rolled around trying to put out the flames. He wasn't even aware he was screaming until he heard Dustin shouting his name.

"Hang on, Malloy!"

Suddenly Dustin was throwing a musty old blanket on him and beating him with those big hands of his. Adelaide's voice joined the echoes in his ears.

"Oh my God, Trevor! Is he all right, Dustin? Is he burned?"

"Call the fire brigade, Adelaide. We need to put this out before the building goes up." Dustin's tone brooked no argument and Trevor heard the click of Adelaide's heels as she hurried away. He could smell clothing and flesh burning, as well as wood and spilled whiskey.

"Damn, who the hell were they?" Dustin helped him sit up and clapped him on the back when he coughed.

Trevor tried to get out of the way of the dinner-plate-sized whacks from Dustin's huge hands, but really he was grateful to Dustin for putting out the flames so he didn't want to insult him. "I don't know, but I knocked one of them out."

"Where?"

"Right there." Trevor pointed to the spot where the smaller man had fallen, but he was gone. Probably hoisted on the shoulder of the big bastard who had lit him on fire. "Son of a bitch."

"No doubt. How many of them were there?" Dustin grabbed a bucket from beside the rain barrel and started tossing water on the burning wagon.

"Two. I've never seen them before, but I've only been in town a little over a month." Trevor coughed again then stood on wobbly legs. The pain in his legs had turned into a throb that threatened his sanity. He reached for another bucket and Dustin yelled at him.

"Sit down, you idiot. In fact, go inside and let Marybeth tend to those burns. I don't need you falling in the damn fire again."

"I didn't fall in the fire, Dustin. That piece of shit set me on fire." Trevor's anger had taken a backseat to his fear and pain, but it was rearing its head again.

"At least he didn't slit your throat first." Dustin kept throwing buckets of water on the fire.

Trevor hadn't even thought about whether or not the two men would kill him. His only thought was to protect Adelaide and her business and damn the consequences. Of course, the consequences were beating a tattoo of pain in his lower extremities.

Adelaide came around the corner followed by the fire brigade. Amongst the bell ringing and people shouting, she zeroed in on him. Trevor was shocked to see tears on her cheeks as she ran toward him and he opened his arms. When he closed his arms around her, it felt so perfect, so *right*. He held her close and murmured soothing words in her ears.

"Are you okay, honey?" he asked.

She let loose a cross between a sob and a laugh. "Me? I'm fine, you big ape. I'm not the one who almost burned to death over some whiskey."

Trevor chuckled. "I did not almost burn to death. Dustin slammed the fire off me."

That made her laugh and cry even harder.

"I'm all right, I swear. I need a few bandages and a beer, but otherwise I'm fine." Trevor gritted out a smile for her and made sure she saw it.

She frowned at him, then at the fire which was quickly coming under control of the well-trained firemen. "Let's get you inside."

Although Trevor protested vigorously at least another dozen times, in the end he gave in to her and hobbled inside. Marybeth was at the ready with everything she needed from hot water to scissors to some awful smelling paste for burns. Fortunately he was wearing a rather old pair of pants that had seen better days so he wasn't too annoyed when she cut them off above the knees. The bottoms were pretty charred and he was damn glad he'd worn canvas pants that day.

If they'd been cotton, he'd probably have lost more than some skin and hair on his calves. Just the thought made his balls crawl up an inch or two.

Marybeth might be rough on the outside, but she took care of him like he was a baby—gently and with a lot of tender loving care. Although the burns had settled into a dull roar of pain, she didn't cause any more pain than absolutely necessary.

Within half an hour, he was cleaned, slathered and bandaged with orders to keep his feet up the rest of the day.

Adelaide went back outside to check with Dustin and the fire brigade. Marybeth pierced Trevor with a gaze that should have made him tremble.

"What happened?"

"Two bastards destroyed part of Adelaide's shipment and tried to kill me. I said that already." Trevor really wanted a nap, but he was embarrassed to admit he needed help up the stairs. That meant he had to listen to whatever was brewing in Marybeth's mind.

"I meant I have never seen Adelaide actually cry before. Not only that, but she was so worried about you, she didn't even think about the fact that she just lost about five hundred dollars worth of booze." Marybeth glared at him. "I'm asking you again, what happened?"

"I fell in love with her."

Well, Jesus Christ on crutches. He certainly hadn't meant to say that out loud.

The moment he realized what he said he wanted to snatch the words back out of the air. Marybeth grinned from ear to ear and rocked back on her heels, her hands neatly folded on her rounded belly. "You don't say?"

"You know I didn't really mean that." Trevor's mouth grew cotton dry and his pulse thundered in his ears, echoing down his throbbing legs.

"Of course you did. It came from the heart—that's why you said it so quickly. Because it's true."

The self-satisfied look on her face was enough to make Trevor's stomach roll like the deck of a ship in the middle of a squall.

"You cannot say anything to Adelaide." Lord, now he sounded desperate.

"What makes you think I'm going to say anything?" Marybeth grinned and waggled her eyebrows.

"Marybeth. Promise me you won't say anything or I'll tell Dustin how you feel."

It was a calculated risk, but apparently a worthwhile one. The grin disappeared off Marybeth's face and she grew just a tad paler.

"What are you talking about?"

Trevor shook his finger at her. "Aha! I knew I was right. You have feelings for that lunkhead. Don't bother denying it now. You said yourself it came from the heart."

"I didn't say a word," she protested.

"But your face did." Trevor knew he had her when she frowned and pursed her lips together.

"Fine, then I won't say anything to Adelaide."

"Won't say anything about what?" Adelaide's husky voice made the hairs on Trevor's arm stand at attention like an army of tiny soldiers.

Shit, shit, shit.

"About how long I have to stay off my feet. She wants me to rest for a week, but I told her one day, no more." Trevor thought he sounded sincere.

Marybeth shot daggers at him with her eyes as he looked at Adelaide and prayed as hard as he could that she'd accept his spoonful of lies. He really, really didn't want to have to explain why he'd told Marybeth what he did.

First of all, he didn't think he could explain it. Secondly, well, he just wasn't ready to.

"I'll be up on my feet tomorrow doing Marybeth's dishes and your sweeping." He finished by smiling his award-winning toothy grin.

Adelaide frowned and looked carefully at his bandaged legs. "We'll see how you feel in the morning. In the meantime, stay here in the kitchen until Dustin can bring you upstairs."

The horror of envisioning Dustin carrying him like a baby made gorge rise up in the back of his throat and stars dance in front of his eyes. "Oh, nooooo. I don't think I'll need help getting up the stairs. No need to bother Dustin."

The indignity of even contemplating that situation was beyond what Trevor would ever allow. It actually made him shudder.

"I'll decide that when I see you walking by yourself. Until then, sit there and let Marybeth get you something hot to drink."

Trevor wasn't about to protest Marybeth serving him. It would be a novelty he'd savor for as long as it lasted. He did, however, use common sense and not flash a self-satisfied grin at the grumpy kitchen mistress. Instead, he just nodded at Adelaide and waited until she left to speak.

"Thank you for not saying anything." He cleared his throat. "About my crazy proclamation. I, ah, appreciate it. A lot."

Marybeth harrumphed and stomped over to the stove to pour a cup of coffee. When she came back and nearly slammed it onto the table, Trevor thanked his lucky stars the hot liquid didn't splash on him. He daren't ask her for a biscuit for fear he'd lose a toe or a finger.

"Just so long as you don't decide to go blabbing what you think you know about me," she threatened with a shake of her fist.

"No need to worry. My lips are sealed."

ꕥ

"You know, I think Marybeth has feelings for Dustin." Trevor made his way slowly up the stairs with Adelaide behind him.

"I've known that a while. Dustin just won't act on it. He figures since he did time in prison, he's no good for any woman." Adelaide knew Trevor was in pain, but he didn't make a sound. She'd pegged him for being a whiny crybaby, and he'd proven her completely wrong. Again.

"Dustin's been in prison?" Trevor sounded quite interested.

"Yes, didn't you know?" Adelaide tucked her arm through Trevor's and encouraged him to keep moving.

Trevor didn't answer the question. "Can I ask what for, or would that be none of my business?"

Adelaide shrugged. "You can ask him if you want. I wouldn't have mentioned it at all, but I thought you knew. He's had a rough time of it in his hometown so he's stayed with me for the last two years since his release. His family isn't...accepting."

She could almost feel Trevor's curiosity dancing up and down on him, but he didn't ask another question. She hid her grin by ducking her head. They reached the top of the stairs in tandem and walked a bit more quickly toward his room. Quick was a relative term though—it was more like a shuffle.

"I wish you had let Dustin car—"

"No!" Trevor cleared his throat. "I mean, no thank you. There's no need for Dustin to strain himself on my account."

Adelaide knew he was lying, but figured it was some kind of manly pride preventing him from accepting Dustin's help. At least he let her lead him up the stairs. When they arrived at Trevor's room, he looked about ready to pass out. His skin was milky white and clammy.

"You need to lie down."

This time he didn't argue, he simply obeyed with some assistance from her. His head hit the pillow and his eyes slammed shut.

"Trevor? Are you okay?"

"Yep. Just felt dizzy and figured since I saw four of you, I needed to shut my eyes for a minute."

Adelaide chuckled and started shifting him farther onto the bed. Since his boots were about destroyed in the fire, he was sock-footed already. She pulled up the quilt from the bottom of the bed and he let out a deep sigh.

"That does feel good. Now all I need is company." He opened one eye and leered. "You busy, pretty lady?"

With a smile and a shake of her head, Adelaide climbed in beside him and snuggled up close. His head naturally fell on her shoulder and she ran her fingers through the soft waves of his hair.

"Mmm, I love the way you smell. Like roses." His words were a bit slurred and she knew he'd be asleep soon. "You always smell so good. Love you, Red."

Trevor's softly spoken words before he drifted off hit Adelaide like a mule kick.

Love you, Red.

Never in her life had she heard those words. Never expected to hear them, especially from someone like Trevor. A man who made his living gambling and telling lies with his eyes.

Holy Mary.

Adelaide lay there for a good long while sorting through the various emotions racing through her. Happiness, despair, disbelief, elation, even a bit of denial. The one thing that kept running through her mind was, did she love him too?

Did she even know what love was? That unnamed emotion that flittered between them, beneath her skin whenever Trevor was around, the clanging in her heart that signaled something different.

Something dangerous.

Something that scared the hell out of her.

She slipped out of bed carefully, making sure Trevor was sleeping comfortably on the pillow. Before she could stop herself, she leaned down and kissed him on the lips. A puff of his breath mixed with hers, a little bit of warmth when she was swimming in cold fear. She pressed her forehead to his and closed her eyes.

Trevor Malloy was trouble with a capital T. If she didn't send him on his way soon, her heart would overtake her common sense.

Chapter Eleven

It had been four days since the fire and Trevor's legs were healed enough to allow him to stand for more than ten minutes at a time. Each day Marybeth took care of his legs and each day he thanked her. Their pact to keep quiet seemed to be working quite nicely.

Adelaide watched him constantly, he felt it. Even when he was sweeping the saloon, her gaze followed him. He wasn't sure why, and it started to make him jittery, as if he needed another excuse. Dustin patrolled the saloon every night with a loaded shotgun. Every man who walked into the saloon was scrutinized and searched before he was allowed to play poker.

The saloon's favorite dealer spent her evenings losing at poker since she was so distracted. Marybeth snapped at everyone and Trevor frowned so much he was getting a crease in his forehead. McGee was keeping them all on edge and Trevor wished he had the courage to wire his family for help.

It was Friday morning when Trevor took the slop bucket from a complaining Marybeth and stepped out into the alley to empty it.

And came face to face with Brett and Noah.

"Holy shit. What are you doing here?" Trevor couldn't contain his surprise. Just when he was thinking about help, his brother and nephew appeared.

"Looking for you, you fool. Mama is about worried sick and somehow Noah here"—Brett cocked his thumb at the younger man—"got it in his head that he wanted to find you. Took us a frigging week to figure out you'd never left Wyoming."

Brett's gaze took in Trevor's outfit from the bandage peeking out from beneath his pant legs, to the apron, to the bucket of slops.

"Good God, Trevor, what the hell are you doing? Are you wearing an apron?"

Trevor felt his cheeks flush and damned Marybeth for forcing him to wear the stupid apron in the first place. Of all the times for Brett to show up, it was when he was being Marybeth's kitchen boy.

Noah's widened eyes drank it all in before he was busy pursing his lips, likely holding back a grin.

With a scowl, Trevor threw the slops into the barrel outside the door with too much force. The slops already in the barrel, which were sold to a local farmer for his pigs, splashed up and a big splat of vile shit landed on his cheek.

Amidst the chuckles and guffaws from his brother and nephew, Trevor dropped the bucket and ripped off the apron. After wiping his face with it, he tossed the white cotton into the bucket. Hands on hips, he contemplated disappearing with Brett and Noah, but knew if Marybeth didn't find him and kill him, Dustin would. Not to mention he wouldn't hurt Adelaide for the world. Leaving without saying goodbye was something he'd never do to her.

"You might as well come in and hear the whole story." Trevor walked back inside, then stopped and glanced behind him. "Grab that bucket, would you, Noah?"

Brett and Noah followed him in, with Noah carrying the bucket and wearing a grin. Marybeth looked up from her daily bread-punching routine to stare at the newcomers.

"One of them looks enough like you to be kin, but the other looks too sweet to be related to you."

Brett nearly hurt himself snorting so hard. Noah kept the grin on his face, but locked the laughter inside. Trevor frowned at his kitchen mistress.

"Marybeth, this snorting hyena is my brother, Brett. The angel is my nephew, Noah. Boys, this is Marybeth and she runs this kitchen with an iron fist. Don't get in her way, say yes ma'am, and always do what she tells you to."

"You are a smart aleck, Trevor. Too quick-tongued for your own good." She shook one dough-covered finger at him. "Where is my apron?"

Brett snorted again with a brief chuckle at the apron question. Trevor gestured to Noah to give him the bucket. When Marybeth caught sight of the apron in the filthy bucket, she pierced him with her razor-sharp gaze.

"It fell in," Trevor offered lamely.

"Next time you'd better dive in after it or I'll make you eat the slops."

"Yes, ma'am." Trevor punched Brett in the arm to make him stop chuckling. It wasn't like Brett to react with laughter and it was beginning to annoy the hell out of Trevor. "You know, big brother, I can kick your ass."

Brett cocked one eyebrow. "Hmph. You tried that once about five years ago. I won."

"There'll be no fighting in here. Why don't you go visit with your family out in the saloon." She waved her arm toward the door. "Later on you can wash my apron."

This time Noah burst out laughing and Trevor did too. It actually was pretty funny—he probably would have thought it funnier if he didn't think Marybeth meant it. She'd done it before and he realized how much he should worship his mother for all the laundry she'd done during his life.

When he opened the kitchen door, Dustin passed by with an armload of liquor. He grunted at Trevor, then stopped to stare at the men behind him.

"My brother and nephew. Relax, big man," Trevor reassured him as they entered the hallway.

Dustin grunted again and continued on into the saloon. "Lovely. More Malloys to muck up my life." They followed behind him.

"Who is that?" Brett asked quietly.

"That's Dustin, the part-time bartender, full-time protector of the woman who owns this saloon." Trevor sat at one of the tables while Brett and Noah looked around.

"Nice place. Clean and neat." High praise from Brett as he joined Trevor.

"No dancing girls?" Noah's brown eyes reflected a bit of disappointment when Trevor shook his head.

"Poker and liquor only, Noah. The girls who serve are awfully nice though." Trevor waggled his eyebrows. "They'll probably fall all over you."

Noah shook his head. "I don't think so. Aunt Rebecca tried to tell me years ago that girls would fly around me like honeybees, but it ain't happened yet."

"You're still a boy with lots of time."

"Maybe." Noah looked skeptical. "Can I ask him for a sarsaparilla?"

"Nicely." Trevor gestured to the bar where Dustin was stocking the bottles. "And don't bring up his time in prison."

Noah gulped and headed over to the bar.

"You really need to stop doing that. Tyler is gonna wipe the floor with you for it." Brett frowned.

"So what? He doesn't even know where I am and he's not looking." Trevor paused. "Right?"

Brett shrugged. "Nicky knew, but Noah left without his pa's permission. I expect he'll come through that door any day."

"Well, shit." Trevor's brother-in-law Tyler Calhoun was a big, bad, son–of-a-bitch ex-bounty hunter with a fast hand and hard-hitting fists. Dustin might be able to give him a good tussle, but Tyler outweighed Trevor by at least fifty pounds. Double damn. "Why are you here anyway?"

"I told you. Mama was worried—you were supposed to let her know where you were and that you were okay."

Trevor had forgotten that promise to his mother, which meant he broke it. Something he'd never done. She'd probably assumed he was dead and an avalanche of guilt landed on his shoulders.

"Hell, I forgot about it. I'll go wire her now." Trevor stood but Brett's hand on his arm stopped him.

"I think you ought to explain what's going on to me first." The seriousness of Brett's expression always gave Trevor pause and this was no exception.

With a dramatic thump, Trevor sat down and folded his hands in front of him. "It all started with a game of poker and a lady dealer named Adelaide."

ꕤ

Penny had been a good girl at one time in her life, but circumstances and her daddy's bad gambling habit sent her down the pathway to hell. That path was paved with whiskey and cards. She'd taken the job at the Last Chance Saloon because she'd heard that Miss Adelaide didn't make the girls work on their backs. However, if an enterprising girl wanted to make some money, she just needed to keep it a secret.

Miss Adelaide was pretty nice compared to some of the other oily sons of bitches Penny'd had the misfortune to work for. Most of them had taken a pound of flesh from her and then kicked her to the curb when someone younger or prettier came along. As long as she did her job, Miss Adelaide treated Penny right proper, with respect and courtesy.

When a customer got out of hand, Dustin protected her and Miss Adelaide gave the man a talking to. Never happened more than once with a customer. It gave her a warm feeling to know she was safe at the Last Chance.

That was, until her daddy got into debt so deep to Buster McGee that Penny's life was again thrown into a pile of shit. Her daddy begged her to do what Buster said or he'd kill him. What could Penny do? She didn't necessarily like her daddy, but she didn't want him dead.

It made her sick to snoop around Miss Adelaide's things, to listen in on conversations and peek through the keyhole at night when Trevor was in her room. That part she liked to do actually. He was a right handsome man, enough to make her nether regions take notice like they'd never done before.

But the snooping and the poking around she didn't like one bit. Then there was Buster's "payment" a couple times a week when Penny told him about what happened at the Last Chance. He always made her suck his little cock and he always smelled like onions. Penny dreamed of having a nice house with a white fence and a couple kids while she did it. It was the only thing that kept her from gagging up her breakfast.

When the two strangers walked in with Trevor, Penny had been lurking in the hallway, listening to Marybeth talk in the kitchen. No one saw her in the shadows, partly because she was tiny and her hair and clothes were dark enough to hide her, and partly because she willed herself to be invisible.

Marybeth had called one of them an angel. Penny watched carefully and nearly gave herself away when she saw him. Tall, broad-shouldered with light brown wavy hair and the most beautiful pair of brown eyes she'd ever laid eyes on. But that wasn't all of it. His face surely did resemble an angel she'd seen in a book once, kind and full of grace he was.

Penny about fell in love with the stranger before she even knew his name. She crept closer to listen, forcing herself to pay attention when all she wanted to do was find out who he was. Her fanciful imagination named him Michael for the archangel who slew the dragon in that book.

More than once Penny had to swallow a sigh.

ഇ൬

Adelaide had slept later than usual that morning. Probably because Trevor woke her in the middle of the night with his soft stroking, and then one thing led to another and they ended up making love twice. After abstaining for four days, they had both hungered.

Making love. That certainly sounded better than fucking. Adelaide wasn't convinced that's what they were doing exactly, but couldn't think of a better way to say it.

Soon she'd send him on his way. Adelaide had honestly not expected him to stay past the first week. She wasn't holding

Trevor hostage, only his pride and honor at the fact that she held his letters. The small scrap of paper sat in the drawer with her unmentionables. Trevor had seen it last week when he wanted her to wear garters and nothing else. He hadn't said anything, but she could feel the conflicting emotions in him when he closed the drawer.

It spoke volumes about his character and where he'd come from. He'd spoken a little about his family, just that he had five brothers and one sister. Made Adelaide wonder if he'd been kicked out by them for something he'd done. His clothes were of good quality, no doubt he could have contacted his family to pay his debt, but he didn't.

The question ran around in her brain. Why?

No answer was forthcoming from the four walls in her bedroom so she finished getting dressed and headed to the stairs. The sound of men's voices drifted up to her. She recognized Trevor and Dustin, but there were two unfamiliar ones. Not wanting to eavesdrop, she hummed as she walked down the stairs.

The talking stopped before she got to the last step. A movement out of the corner of her eye caught her attention and she yelped in surprise. No wonder with her nerves being frayed the way they were. Within seconds, four angry males converged on the shadow behind her.

They dragged Penny out, looking scared enough to pee her knickers.

"Stop! It's Penny. Let her go." Adelaide pulled at Dustin's arm.

All of them let go at once and Penny bolted for the door. One of the strangers, the bigger one who resembled Trevor quite a bit, caught her by the waist. She dangled like a fish on a hook with her legs going a mile a minute.

"Easy, little girl. I won't hurt you." His voice was deeper, huskier than Trevor's.

"I'm not a little girl. Miss Adelaide, please tell him to let me go. I didn't mean no harm. I was just... I... Please let me go." Penny burst into tears, yet the stranger simply gazed at Adelaide with one eyebrow cocked.

Adelaide walked over to him and looked Penny in the eye. "Please, set her down." When Penny's feet hit the floor, she started to run but Adelaide's hand on her arm stopped her. "Where are you going?"

Tears streamed down the girl's face. "I'm sorry, Miss Adelaide. I didn't mean no harm."

With her arm around the girl's shoulder, Adelaide led her over to the table and eased her into a chair. "It's okay, Penny. What were you doing?"

"I didn't want to do it. Honest. I ain't a snoop, but my daddy got in trouble so I had to." Penny trembled so hard the chair vibrated.

Trevor growled, "What the hell does that mean?"

Adelaide frowned at Trevor. "I don't think we need to scare her any more than she already is." She crouched down and took Penny's frigid hands in her own. "You are a good girl. I'm sure whatever has happened isn't your fault. Why don't you sit here and Dustin will get a cup of tea?"

With a disgusted sigh from somewhere near his toes, Dustin stomped off to the kitchen. "I'll get the damn tea."

"Who is she?" the first stranger asked.

"One of the serving girls. Her name is Penny. Sweet thing, kind of timid like a little mouse." Trevor put his hands on his hips. "A little mouse with big ears apparently. And perhaps a big mouth."

Adelaide stood and stared at Trevor. "Now how about you tell me who these men are and why the hell you jumped on her like a pack of dogs?"

"We didn't jump on her. Okay, maybe we did, but not like a pack of dogs. We were protecting you in case you didn't notice." Trevor almost looked like a little boy with his lip pooched out.

"And these men are who?"

The stranger who'd caught Penny never broke his gaze, never even twitched an inch. A cold man who didn't let much affect him.

"This is my brother, Brett Malloy, and my nephew, Noah Calhoun." Trevor pointed to them as he introduced them. "This is Adelaide Burns, my..." He trailed off, staring at Adelaide with confusion in his eyes.

Adelaide stuck out her hand. "I'm Adelaide Burns, the owner of the Last Chance and Trevor's boss."

Both men doffed their hats and shook her hand lightly, their skin covered in the same calluses that graced Trevor. Obviously a working family.

"She's not just my boss," Trevor interjected. "She's my friend, the woman who can beat me at poker, and...my lover." Trevor finished by wrapping his arm around her shoulder.

Adelaide's mouth dropped open. Never in a hundred years had she expected to hear Trevor say that to his family. She didn't know whether to be embarrassed or flattered. Who knew what his family thought about her after hearing that? Gramps wouldn't have cared a flying fart if she had a lover, but Trevor's family might feel differently.

Brett simply nodded. "Figured it was a woman."

That remark stung. Adelaide did not want to be lumped in with a thousand other women who likely threw themselves at

Trevor's feet. No doubt he'd never had a problem finding a woman to spark with, or fall into his bed.

"Don't be an ass, Brett. She's not just a woman." He flicked his gaze to hers. "She's *my* woman."

Adelaide's heart raced so fast, she knew the others must hear it. Trevor nearly turned her into a puddle with his words. Almost as if he didn't know what he was going to say, like he'd let his heart do the talking. In fact, he sounded a bit surprised by what he had said.

Penny and Noah watched Adelaide and Trevor with wide eyes. Adelaide wanted to drag Trevor upstairs and make him explain everything he'd just said. Unfortunately, she couldn't do that. Instead, she pointed at the chairs.

"Now that the introductions are over, sit down. Let's find out what's going on."

Like a pack of now well-trained dogs, they all sat. Adelaide circled the table, looking at all of them in turn. She decided to start with Trevor's family.

"What are you doing here?"

Brett's cheek twitched and Noah's cheeks colored. Interesting reaction.

"We came to find my brother, ma'am. He's been gone without a word for more than a month and our mama was pretty worried about him." Brett spoke without much inflection in his voice. His eyes were like a frozen pond in December. "I understand he lost a good deal of money to you in a poker game."

Adelaide wanted to hear an accusation in his voice, but she didn't. However, she was damn certain that's what he was doing quite stealthily. Brett was a dangerous man.

"That's true. He threw in his letters for five thousand dollars. I won the pot and he owed that money to me." She couldn't put it more plainly than that. Waiting for the snide comments, she steeled herself to protect her heart.

"Sounds like something Trevor would do. I apologize for his stupidity, ma'am. We'd be happy to pay you the money." Brett's expression hadn't changed, but Adelaide sensed an easing of his distrust.

"You are not going to pay my debt, big brother. Not a chance." Trevor frowned fiercely.

Brett never even glanced at Trevor, he kept his gaze on Adelaide, waiting for her answer.

"I was worried about him, too, ma'am." The younger man, Noah, spoke in a quiet tone. "Uncle Trevor needs to come home."

Adelaide gazed into Trevor's eyes and saw need, confusion, and God help her, love.

"Trevor needs to make that decision himself."

Trevor opened his mouth to speak when Dustin came back with a tin mug. He thrust it at Penny. "Here, drink this. Marybeth put some honey and lemon in it."

Penny took the mug with shaking hands and a whispered thank you. Adelaide wanted Trevor to continue, but knew the moment was past. She turned her attention to her wayward serving girl.

"Now, Penny, what were you doing?"

Penny's small hands wrapped around the mug and she sipped the hot liquid. "Just listening."

Trevor slapped the table hard. "And who did you tell about what you heard?"

Penny jumped. "Buster McGee," she whispered.

"Son of a bitch," Trevor shouted. "What the hell for?"

Penny snuffled and seemed to shrink down within herself. "I'm sorry, Miss Adelaide. I had to save my daddy's miserable hide from that shyster, Buster McGee. He wanted to know what you all were doing over here, even in...even in your bedroom."

Trevor cursed and Brett's cold gaze nearly froze poor Penny in her chair. Dustin frowned at the little black-haired waif.

"Why would you be putting a knife in Miss Adelaide's back?" It was like Dustin to cut to the heart of the matter like that.

"I didn't mean no harm. I'll pack up my things and go, take my worthless daddy out of town." She took a shaky breath. "You been so kind to me, I...I'm sorry for what I done." Her expression regarded Adelaide with sincere regret.

"It's okay, Penny." Adelaide patted her shoulder, resisting the urge to hug her.

"It sure as hell isn't okay," Trevor groused. "She's been peeking in your bedroom, Adelaide."

Oh, she'd missed that part. Penny must've had an eyeful. No doubt McGee knew what color her damn nipples were by now. Why the hell was he using Penny? What information did he hope to gain?

"Why did he want you to watch me, Penny?"

Penny shrugged. "I dunno. He just did. I'll be grateful not to see him twice a week." She made a disgusted face. "He's a pig."

The air around them changed while the men digested what she'd said, then came to the same conclusion as Adelaide. Information wasn't the only thing Buster was taking from Penny.

Adelaide swore Brett's face turned to stone, Trevor looked furious, Dustin looked murderous and even Noah looked ready to do harm. Put a damsel in distress and all the knights come charging.

"You have two choices, Penny. Stay here and we'll protect you, or leave town with your daddy and get as far away as possible before McGee finds out." Trevor did have a brain in his good-looking noggin. It was exactly what Adelaide was going to suggest.

Penny peered up at Trevor with her huge brown eyes and blinked. "Leave town? Where would I go?"

"Don't matter. Just as long as you're safe," Noah stated softly.

Adelaide saw Penny's face light up when Noah spoke to her. So that was the way the wind blew. He was a good-looking young man and if he was Trevor's nephew, Adelaide would bet he was a good man too.

"You don't have to leave, Penny. You can stay right here," Adelaide reassured her.

"But what about my daddy?"

"Tell him to go to hell," Brett said in a low voice. "No man uses his daughter's body to pay his gambling debts." Brett voiced aloud what everyone present thought of Penny's father. Probably a good thing he wasn't within striking distance.

Penny shrank from the cold fierceness in Brett's tone. That brought her closer to Noah, who patted her shoulder. Pretty soon Penny's infatuation would turn to obsession if she wasn't careful. Adelaide knew of which she spoke.

"I think we should just confront him and be done with it."

Adelaide's words fell like stones in a calm pond. She could almost see the ripples floating through the room as the idea hit each man in turn. Penny appeared plumb confused.

"What are you talking about?" Trevor asked with narrowed eyes.

"I want to confront that bastard McGee and put an end to whatever he plans on doing. He's not that smart, between the brains in this room, we should be able to come up with a plan to confront him, stop him and get rid of him." As she spoke, Adelaide's voice gained strength. "I'm tired of wondering what he's going to do next. Obviously he'll kill us if he can. I say we stop him before he has another chance."

Trevor grabbed her elbow and steered her out of the saloon with a curt, "We'll be back," directed at the others.

Most times, Trevor's temper simmered beneath the surface. It took a great deal to actually get him riled. This was one of those times he was absolutely furious.

And his anger was directed at the woman he loved.

They went into her small office, well more or less he shoved her into the office and slammed the door. She wrenched her elbow out of his grasp and stepped away from him. He thought for a moment she was going to haul off and punch him.

"How dare you?" Her hazel eyes snapped sparks. "You have no right to push me around. Ever."

Trevor put his hands on his hips and took a deep breath before he said something that would put a nail or two in his coffin. "I'm sorry for that. I do things sometimes without thinking."

"You should be sorry."

Obviously when Adelaide was angry, the world knew about it. Her words could probably cut barbed wire.

"Listen, Red, Dustin and I have been patrolling the saloon twenty-four hours a day for a week. I won't—I mean I can't let you put yourself in any danger," Trevor tried to explain. "Let us handle that son of a bitch. After all, he tried to kill me."

Adelaide poked her finger into his chest. Hard. "You will not tell me what I can or can't do. I already told you I don't run from battles. I stand and fight for me and mine. There's no way in hell I would allow you to 'protect' me while I cowered in the shadows."

Trevor ran his hands through his hair in frustration. "Damn, you're just like Lily."

That seemed to catch Adelaide's attention. "Who's Lily?"

"Another stubborn woman who yanked me into her wild plans, which could have cost both of us our lives."

With narrowed eyes, Adelaide pushed at his shoulder. "I asked you a question. You compare me to some woman, I want to know why. Who is Lily?"

"My oldest brother's wife. Lily concocted this scheme in San Francisco to rescue my niece and well, the details aren't important. She took her life in her hands and there wasn't a damn thing I could do to stop her." Trevor still had a smidge of resentment about it too, not that he'd ever tell Lily or Ray. "I'll be damned if I let you put yourself into that kind of danger."

Her nostrils flared, her eyes blazed and Trevor's heart beat a steady rhythm that flowed through his body. Instead of being angry and frustrated, he was aroused as all get out. In fact, he wanted to push her against the wall and pull her skirt up.

"Dustin knows better than to assume I will hide. You should too. We'll do this together or you can get on your pony and get the hell out of Cheyenne. Trevor, are you listening to me?"

"I can't go through this again." Trevor's heart pinched at the thought of something happening to Adelaide.

"It's not your choice."

"Dammit, Red! Don't make me choose. It was hard enough with Lily, and I didn't love her!"

After Trevor's announcement, the silence in the small room was thick.

"You love me?" Her voice was so quiet he barely heard her. He couldn't tell what she was thinking because her eyes were shuttered.

"It wasn't exactly how I wanted to say it, but yes, I do love you. I...I've never done this before and obviously I'm a complete idiot because I did it wrong." Trevor stopped talking before he put both feet in his mouth.

"I...I don't know what to say." Adelaide had never looked so unsure of herself.

"Tell me you won't put yourself in danger."

He wasn't expecting her to punch him, but damned if she didn't haul off and do it. His head snapped back from the blow and he thought he tasted a bit of blood from a cut on his cheek.

"Why did you do that?"

"You are a son of a bitch, Malloy. Trying to make me do what you want by handing me your standard shit about loving me. I can't believe you would sink that low." Heat and hurt came off her in waves.

Trevor experienced his own measure of hurt that she thought he was lying. "I would never, ever tell a woman I loved her to get into her bed or trick her into doing something. In fact, I've never told a woman I loved her."

She must have seen something in his eyes because she blinked rapidly then frowned. Trevor's control broke—to hell with the folks waiting out in the saloon. He had to taste her, to brand her until he was the only man Adelaide would know. The only man to ever be in her bed again.

When he stepped toward her, she licked her lips, making his cock twitch. Adelaide's mouth was an amazing tool that she knew how to wield like a master. Trevor cupped her cheeks and descended without another word. Their lips met in a hot clash of skin, rubbing, moaning and tasting each other. Within seconds, their mouths opened and tongue rasped against tongue. Rapid licks of pleasure coursed through him, igniting every inch of his skin. Her hands grasped at him, pulling him closer until they were pressed together.

"Trevor? What the hell is going on in there?" Brett's voice came from the other side of the door.

The couple locked in a sensual haze of primal heat didn't stop and didn't answer.

Bam, bam, bam.

"Open the damn door, pretty boy." Dustin sounded angry. "You don't want me to knock it down."

Trevor broke his connection with Adelaide's mouth long enough to growl, "Go away."

Pushing her against the wall, Trevor cupped her breasts, rubbing his thumbs against the hardened nipples that seemed to beg for attention. She moaned into his mouth and the sound went straight to his hardened staff.

"Adelaide, are you okay?" Marybeth joined in the party listening outside the door. "It sounds like she's in pain."

"She ain't in pain. That there was a bedroom moan," Penny piped up.

Trevor wrenched away from Adelaide and looked into her amused eyes. "I might have to shoot all of them."

Adelaide giggled and touched his lips with one finger. Trevor licked at her skin and was rewarded with a hitching breath.

"You'd better open the door."

It was the last thing Trevor wanted to do, but he did it anyway because Adelaide told him to. When he swung open the door, five people nearly fell onto his feet.

"This isn't a peep show. We'll be back out in a few minutes."

Dustin glared at Trevor and shot a narrow-eyed look at Adelaide. "Couple of goddamn bunnies." He walked away leaving Marybeth grinning, Penny nodding and Brett looking exasperated. Noah was the only one who appeared confused.

"Can we finish this without you taking it out of your trousers?" Brett said sharply.

Trevor glanced at Adelaide and knew the moment had been lost, although the arousal still simmered beneath the surface. He gestured for her to precede him out the door.

"Fine, let's talk about what we're going to do." Trevor wanted to punch Brett for being so damn bossy all the time.

"Need to buy you a chastity belt." Brett kept right on being snide.

"Mind your business, big brother. You're stepping over the line," Trevor warned.

He put his hand at the small of Adelaide's back as they all trooped back into the saloon. Her scent remained in his nose, the ghost of her touch on his lips and the weight of his heart in her hands.

Chapter Twelve

In his bedroom on the second floor of the Silver Spittoon, McGee looked down at the whore currently sucking his dick and realized he was tired of her. The mechanical way she used her mouth pissed him off. He yanked at her hair.

"Do it right, girlie, or you will be sorry you got up this morning," he snarled.

She started using her tongue, rather than risk McGee's wrath. Good thing too, he had no patience for stupid whores.

"McGee?" a man called through the closed door.

"If you don't want to be dead, you'd better fucking leave." McGee tried to concentrate on a cock-sucking that was getting better by the minute.

"I'm out."

McGee recognized the voice outside the door as Kincaid. The gunslinger had proved to be a disappointment, not taking the job right away and jabbering on about figuring things out first. It was all a crock of shit.

"Come in then."

The door opened and Kincaid strolled in with barely a glance at the redheaded slut on her knees.

"Am I interrupting something?"

McGee sneered. "Speak your piece."

"I decided not to take the job." Kincaid kept his hands resting on his pistols. "Thought I ought to tell you."

"Fucking coward." McGee's temper flared to life. "Should've put a bullet in you, too."

The smile that Kincaid gave him was almost frightening, almost but not quite.

"I'd like to see you try, fat man."

There was one thing he realized at that moment. Kincaid might not want the job, but he could kill a man easily.

"Fine then, get on with ya. I'll find someone else to do the job. I still think you're a fucking yellow-bellied coward." McGee waved his hand in the direction of the door. "Don't let the door hit you in the ass on the way out."

Kincaid glanced at the girl, then at McGee. Without another word, he stepped out of the room and closed the door.

McGee smacked the back of the whore's stupid head. "Get busy, you cow."

ഊ

In the end, Adelaide agreed to take part in the plan, but didn't promise Trevor she wouldn't put herself in danger. She didn't know if it was what she wanted to do, and she wondered if she'd change her mind. They sat planning the details most of the afternoon until patrons started trickling through the door.

One of them was Kincaid.

Dustin immediately jumped from behind the bar; Trevor looked amazed that the big man had the agility. Dustin's bulk blocked Kincaid's path. With an easy smile, the gunman raised his hands, showing he had no weapons.

"Easy there, big fella. I just came to talk."

Dustin's expression and position didn't change. Trevor came up beside the two men and folded his arms over his chest. "So talk."

Kincaid gazed over Trevor's shoulder. "To her."

She'd been quiet, but when Trevor turned around and looked at her, she could tell he'd known she was there. His expression told her he wasn't happy about Kincaid's request, however Trevor kept silent. His lips were pressed so tightly together, they resembled a white line. He didn't want her in danger, he'd made that clear. The decision remained hers.

"Sit down and talk, Mr. Kincaid. You've got five minutes before my manners go away." Adelaide gestured to an empty table in the corner by the stairs. Kincaid inclined his head and walked toward the table.

"Why the hell did you let him in?" Trevor hissed. "He's probably got a little pistol tucked down his pants to shoot you in the heart with."

"I don't care what's in his pants." Adelaide frowned at him. "Haven't you heard the expression keep your friends close and your enemies closer? I want to know what he's up to."

As she approached the table, Kincaid took off his hat and set it on the chair next to him. Trevor glared at it and pushed it aside to sit down heavily, Colt .45 resting comfortably in his hand. Kincaid merely smiled and picked up his hat off the floor.

"Your guard dog has a temper, Miss Adelaide."

Adelaide thought she heard Trevor growl. "He's concerned about me, rightly so, Mr. Kincaid. You and your men have tried to kill me and mine, and destroyed my property. You can understand why we're not too friendly."

"I've done nothing to hurt you, ma'am."

Trevor slammed his fist on the table. "That's a load of shit. Want to see the goddamn mark on her scalp where the bullet parted her hair or the scars on my legs from the fire those two bastards set?"

Kincaid didn't flinch. "I haven't done a thing."

"Then who did?" Adelaide asked.

The dark-haired gunman shook his head. "I don't know who it was. I was contacted to do a job, but I refused it."

"Are we supposed to believe that?" Trevor snorted.

"I don't care if you believe me or not." Kincaid looked at Adelaide. "I appreciated the way you treated me, so I thought I'd return the favor and warn you."

"He's trying to set you up." Trevor stood. "I think his five minutes are up, Red."

"Sit down, Trevor. Let the man speak." Adelaide wanted to hear what Kincaid had to say.

Although his expression was mutinous, Trevor shut his mouth and leaned back in his chair, cradling the gun.

Kincaid's mouth twitched, as if fighting a grin. "Thank you, Miss Adelaide."

"You have about two minutes left." Even if Adelaide wanted to hear what he had to say, she was no fool and she wouldn't allow him to treat her like one.

"McGee hired me to kill you."

Hearing it said out loud was like a slap in the face for Adelaide. She gritted her teeth to swallow back the cry that wanted to burst from her throat. "Go on."

"He wanted it done as quickly as possible, any way I could. I told him I didn't work that way." Kincaid shrugged. "He tried to push me, even offered me that little black-haired serving girl of yours."

A curse from behind them made Adelaide aware that Brett had joined them. “Who the hell is this?”

Trevor didn’t look at his brother. “Shut up and listen, Brett.”

Adelaide wouldn’t have been so blunt, but that’s what she wanted the older Malloy to do.

“McGee got tired of waiting for me, hired a few others. That’s when I told him no.” Kincaid’s gaze bored into Adelaide’s. Behind his eyes she saw the remnants of a man who was once good, perhaps a man with a sister or a mother he couldn’t protect. A man who had gone down the path of wrong for so long, he couldn’t even see the path of right. Although he hungered for it.

“Who are the others?”

Kincaid nodded at a blond man standing at the bar chatting with one of the girls. “That there is Fontaine and the dark Mexican playing poker over yonder is Gomez. Either one of them will slit your throat for fifty bucks.”

Adelaide couldn’t stop the shudder from wracking her body. So close. Those damn killers were so close and she had no idea they were there. Sons of bitches.

“Thanks for the information. We’ll take care of them.” Adelaide sounded surer than she felt at that moment, which was scared. Dustin squeezed her shoulder and headed off to take out the trash that littered her saloon.

“He’ll send more.” Kincaid’s tone left no doubt he was telling the truth.

“We’re going to get rid of McGee so he won’t bother us anymore.” Just saying it out loud made Adelaide feel better.

Kincaid nodded. “Just don’t get your neck stretched over that piece of shit.”

"Why are you helping me?" Adelaide wasn't about to let him leave without telling her that.

"I can't rightly say. I reckon it's because of the way you treat folks, even those who work for you. McGee has no call to gun you down. You're taking away his piece of the pie, Miss Adelaide, and he wants it back." Kincaid stood, followed by Trevor whose gun never left his palm. "Thank you for the hospitality."

With a tip of his hat, Kincaid walked out of the Last Chance Saloon. Adelaide wondered if she'd ever see him again, and if he'd ever regret not seeing his job done. A shiver snaked up her spine and Trevor's warm arm landed on her shoulders.

"Good riddance," Trevor snarled like a chained dog wanting to chase the enemy.

"He did me a kindness, Trevor. I won't forget that."

Trevor snorted. "As far as I'm concerned, he could've been lying to you from the minute he walked in here. In fact, he could have a rifle pointed at your head right now."

It was all true. Not only that, it was possible. Kincaid looked like the kind of man who would lie to get what he wanted, no matter what. However, something inside Adelaide told her he wasn't lying. That her courtesy and her kindness struck a chord inside the cold gunman.

"Now are you going to tell me who that was?" Brett piped up from behind them.

"That's the gunman hired to kill Adelaide."

Adelaide never expected Brett to show any emotion beside anger, but his face reflected complete shock and surprise. "What? And you let him sit at the table like you're having Sunday fucking tea?"

Tired of men trying to control her life, Adelaide's anger nearly boiled over. She walked over to Brett and poked one finger into his hard chest. "That was my choice, nobody *lets* me do anything. This is my saloon and I'm the boss. Period. End of discussion. You don't like that, the door is that way."

She clenched her fists and went to the kitchen to get something to eat. To hell with the men standing in the saloon like her own personal guard.

"She's bossy."

Trevor cocked one eyebrow at his brother. "That she is. And I don't think that's ever going to change."

"How can you stand it?" Brett walked over to the bar and asked Dustin for a whiskey.

Trevor considered Brett's question and found that he didn't have an answer. It wasn't something that he withstood or even contemplated outside of Adelaide herself. Her bossiness was part of her personality; it couldn't be separated and scrutinized to be discarded. Adelaide wouldn't be herself if she wasn't bossy.

Somehow his thoughts helped him calm down enough to put the gun back in its holster. He was still angry with Adelaide for letting Kincaid sit and talk to them, but knew it was her decision to make. Her life and her saloon were at stake.

Trevor had come to respect everything Adelaide did to be who she was and remain a woman. Took a lot of guts and courage, something she had an abundance of. Something that Trevor loved her for.

Even if he wanted to lock her away to keep her safe from harm. He joined Brett in a drink all the while keeping his eye on the other patrons in the saloon. The urge to protect Adelaide grew stronger, as did his need to touch her, feel her and bring some peace to the demons dancing on his shoulder.

Soon he couldn't stand it any longer so he went to find her. Trevor opened the kitchen door to see Adelaide drinking coffee by the window. The sun streaming in lit her hair like a halo of fire, sending shimmers of longing through him. Her shoulders stiffened when he stepped up behind her.

When he touched her lightly, she jumped.

"Did you come in here to tell me what to do? Or tell me what a fool I am?" Her voice shook with quiet anger.

"Neither." Trevor kissed the side of her neck. "I came in here to seduce you."

She snorted a laugh. "You're not very subtle, Trevor Malloy."

Her scent filled his nose and the small hairs on his arms grew rigid with goose bumps. The heat of her skin coated his lips, a delicious taste that made him hungry for more. More of everything. He licked and sucked at her neck.

"Did you know that all redheads are supposed to be descended from Prince Idon of Mu?"

Adelaide took a shuddering breath. "What are you talking about?"

"He was the Prince of Atlantis." Trevor wrapped his arms around her waist and pulled her sweet ass against his throbbing erection. "Apparently, it was sunset when he found Atlantis and the colors were so beautiful, he wanted to save red-colored beauty for everyone. His wish came true when his hair turned red and his face covered in freckles."

Trevor kissed the freckles on her cheek as he reached for her bountiful breasts. "So every time you see a redhead, you see the first sunset in Atlantis. You, my darlin', are a princess, descended from the king of redheads."

He pinched her nipples and she moaned low in her throat.

"You are too charming, too smooth, for the likes of me. Why don't you seduce a woman worthy of your skills?"

"I don't want anyone else." He sounded hoarse and needy, even to his own ears. "I want my redheaded princess. I want *you.*"

"I am no princess. Jesus, I'm just a Mick gambler who got lucky."

He cupped her breasts, feeling their weight, aching to taste them. "Mmmm... All I care about is that you are here now. In my arms."

"You need to take that out of my kitchen." Marybeth's voice cut through the sensual fog crowding Trevor's brain.

He laughed against Adelaide's neck. "Let's go upstairs."

Without a word, she took his hand and led him out of the kitchen. Trevor tried hard to ignore Marybeth's snickering. He didn't want to think about anything but the incredible woman in front of him.

Adelaide's arousal overshadowed her anger. She felt like she was caught in a twister, spinning around and around. It didn't matter where she went, someone was always trying to take what she rightfully owned. Granddaddy had taught her to stand on her own two feet.

But Trevor's warm hands felt as good as heaven right about now.

His scent, his heat, his essence surrounded her, enveloped her. She was helpless to stop her reaction and dammit all, she didn't want to stop it.

Trevor was exactly what she needed. Adelaide trembled with mixed emotions as they headed upstairs to her bedroom. She honestly didn't care what folks thought of them going off alone. She focused on her heartbeat and the steady thrum of excitement rushing through her veins. The small hairs on her body rose, knowing Trevor climbed behind her—close enough that she felt his breath on her neck. She swallowed and tried to tell herself to calm down, but it was no use.

When they reached her room, Adelaide walked in, controlling the urge to hurry. Trevor followed at a slower pace, closing the door behind him. The heat from his gaze hit her like the afternoon sun, raising her temperature even further. The snick of the key in the lock was like a caress.

Yes.

Adelaide unbuttoned her dress and shed her clothes without much finesse. Her body urged her to hurry. By the time she crawled into bed, Trevor was as naked as she. Without a word, he took her in his arms and Adelaide stopped thinking. Skin on skin, flesh on flesh, hunger to hunger.

The heat between them was scorching. Enough to send her temperature up and make her pussy even wetter. The roughness of his body hair rubbed against her skin each time she moved. She touched his back, feeling the muscle, sinew and bone beneath her questing fingers.

"God you feel good," he mumbled against her collarbone as his tongue swept along the skin.

"Mmm, so do you."

Adelaide nibbled on his shoulder, darker now from the outdoor work, a few freckles dotted the skin. She smiled and didn't mention it for fear his manly pride might be hurt. Instead she grabbed his amazingly firm ass and squeezed, pulling him closer. He felt remarkable, perfect. His hard cock nestled nicely on her stomach and his balls landed on her pussy. So hot.

"Careful, honey, that's dangerous territory."

She opened her legs and pushed her hungry body against him. "Show me how dangerous."

He rocked slowly and Adelaide's body clenched in pleasure. She needed this desperately. Needed to reaffirm life and the man in her arms. Trevor kissed his way down her chest to her breasts where he licked each one in turn, thoroughly. When he bit them, a sizzling bolt flew through her body and even her toes tingled.

"Do it again," she commanded.

"As you wish." Trevor inched her legs apart and one hand crept down to her aching center. Adelaide watched as his scorching mouth closed around one nipple, captured by the sight of her pale breast and pink areola disappearing into his mouth. When his white teeth nibbled on the hardened peak, she nearly came from the pleasure and pain racing through her. His finger circled her aching clit, making her squirm, making her want his mouth there instead.

"Trevor?"

"Hm?" He switched nipples and started finger fucking her. Tremors snaked through her and she held on, waiting to come.

"I want you to lick me."

"I am. Can't you"—he swiped his tongue up and down her right nipple eliciting a body wide shiver—"feel me?"

Oh, hell, of course she felt him. "Not there."

He looked up at her and sucked on her nipple, the erotic intensity of the moment sent a rush of abandon through her. Trevor grinned with the pink bud lightly clenched in his teeth.

"Ah, you want me to move south? Yes, ma'am. That's definitely on the menu." With a wicked glint in his eyes, Trevor moved down her body, both hands pinching her nipples as he kissed, bit and licked her overheated skin. It was sweet, sweet torture.

Adelaide spread her legs wider, anticipating the pleasure to be had. She throbbed in tune with her heartbeat. He pushed his face into her auburn curls and blew—the cool air of his breath contrasting sharply with the heat of her pussy.

"God, Trevor, don't make me wait any longer."

The slightest touch of his tongue made Adelaide jerk. She couldn't get much wetter or hotter without coming, and she wanted his mouth on her while she did it.

"You taste good, like a woman who wants to be pleasured." One hand continued to pleasure her breasts while the other traveled down to slide under her ass and cup her. She didn't understand what he was doing until his thumb pressed into her while his tongue laved her hot button.

Oh God, yes.

Nimble touches, feathery caresses and tweaks had her aching for more. Desperation almost overcame her. She needed him. Now. "Please."

Trevor seemed to understand her needs because his thumb went deeper inside her, sliding in and out. He sucked her clit, then nibbled, then licked, then back to sucking hard. With each pull of his mouth, her body throbbed harder.

Yes, yes, yes.

"Oh God, Trevor, I'm close."

One finger slid into her tight ass and the combination of his mouth and his hand sent her over a precipice of pleasure. Waves of sensation crashed and her body jerked with each one.

He held on, still sucking and licking her, until the final ripple subsided. One last long swipe with his tongue made her jump with remembered ecstasy.

Adelaide felt like a rag doll, limp with bliss. She could only watch him, his erection jutting proudly from between his legs. His fiery gaze traveled over her as his hand squeezed his cock. Unbelievably, a jolt of arousal hit her like a bullet. The sight of this beautiful man pleasuring himself on her bed was enough to send her back into a needful state.

He smiled when he noticed her watching him. "You like this?"

"God yes." Before she even thought about it, her hand was on her pussy, rubbing her over-sensitized clit. She jerked at her own touch.

His pupils dilated when he saw what she was doing. "I like that, too." His voice was husky with arousal.

Adelaide flipped over until she was on her hands and knees in front of him. She licked the head of his cock as his hand continued to move up and down his staff. The muscles in his thighs trembled as she pushed his hand away, allowing her full access. Taking him in her mouth, she cupped his balls and caressed them. Trevor's moan echoed through the room.

She took him as far in her mouth as she could, until he touched the back of her throat and he jerked in response.

"Jesus, Red..." His voice was so hoarse, she barely understood him.

Her tongue darted around the base each time her mouth slid down. Trevor tasted like man, like pure pleasure. The throbbing member in her power was as hard as a tree. When her teeth grazed the head, he pulled her back.

"I need to fuck you." She understood his urgency as it echoed through her body. Within seconds, he was behind her, pushing his hot, wet cock into her grasping pussy. "I can't... I need... Ah, God..."

Trevor drove in hard and fast, burying himself inside her deeply. For a moment, an endless moment, he paused while she clenched around him. He was so hard, so damn hard, so damn good. Adelaide was no shrinking virgin, but she'd never felt a man as hard or thick as Trevor. He slid in and out, slowly at first. Tingles raced around with each thrust, her body climbing the pinnacle of pleasure with him.

The room filled with the scent of their loving, the sound of flesh against flesh, quiet moans and hitched breaths. Adelaide thrust against him, driving him deeper, harder. Until her body tightened and tightened and she knew she would reach another peak.

As Trevor's tempo picked up speed, he grasped her hips, pulling them closer together as he pushed into her. She closed her eyes and let the euphoria overtake her body, stars dancing behind her lids. He roared her name as he buried himself inside her, and his warm seed spilled within. Adelaide followed behind him, the lush orgasm spreading through her, roaring through until her ears rang and her skin sang.

Trevor kissed her back and helped her boneless body onto the bed, then spooned against her. He was still nestled inside her, still hard, the beat of his pulse rhyming with hers.

Adelaide closed her eyes. Regardless of the outside world, she allowed peace to steal through her and reveled in the feel of Trevor's arms around her.

Chapter Thirteen

"Are you ready?"

Trevor's voice cut through Adelaide's thoughts as she sat brooding in her office. She shook her head to clear it and rubbed her hands on the front of her skirt. If she didn't know any better, she'd have thought she was nervous. Ridiculous of course. Adelaide was never nervous.

Determined. That's what she felt. Determined to force McGee's hand and get rid of the dark threatening cloud that hung over her and the Last Chance Saloon.

"Ready." She took a deep breath and stood. Trevor looked so serious, Adelaide smiled. "Don't worry, Malloy. This will work."

"I don't care if it works or not. I just want you to be safe."

Now that was the kind of thing that would make her heart turn into a puddle of jelly. She gave him a tight smile and touched his arm.

"Brett and Noah will stay here and watch the saloon while we're gone," Trevor said and continued to gaze at her with such a serious face. "Let's go beard the lion then."

Dustin waited outside the door. He frowned even deeper than Trevor. Between the two of them, Adelaide felt like she was at a funeral, not a challenge.

"Oh, for pity's sake. Both of you stop it. He's not going to shoot me dead if I walk into his saloon." Adelaide ignored the shudder that raced down her spine at the thought. She refused to be afraid. McGee wasn't worth the effort.

The three of them left the saloon together, stepping out into the evening light. Purple laced the clouds, giving the sky a bruised appearance. The warmth of the sun had dissipated, leaving a cool bite to the air. Adelaide took Trevor's arm and inched marginally closer to him. He glanced down at her with a question in his eyes.

She shook her head and kept walking. With a stiff spine, Adelaide headed for The Silver Spittoon. A few men standing outside scattered like the insects they resembled. When Adelaide reached the door, Dustin held it open and she walked in.

The coldness hit her first. She'd never been inside before, and the welcoming presence she was used to from her own saloon was missing. Then there was the smell. A mixture of dirt, sweat, stale whiskey and something else indefinable. Altogether, a rancid odor that made Adelaide wrinkle her nose and hold her breath.

Fontaine and Gomez stood at the bar and sneered at Adelaide, Trevor and Dustin. More than likely, the two little bastards wanted some revenge since they'd been kicked out of the Last Chance Saloon and hadn't been allowed back in.

Adelaide knew she represented everything McGee wasn't and successfully earned what he tried to hang onto by brute force. He was a bully, plain and simple. The cowboys and other folks in The Silver Spittoon all had a haunted look to them, empty eyes with no life in them. No hope.

Adelaide took a deep breath and walked as gracefully as she could deeper into the room. McGee was nowhere to be seen, but that didn't deter her. A man behind the filthy wooden bar sneered at her, his Chinese face more at home on the docks of San Francisco than in Cheyenne.

"What you want, girl?" He turned and spat onto the floor.

"Tell McGee to get his ass out here." Adelaide spoke with enough authority that the Chinese man started a bit. Good. He ought to be afraid of her. She was angry enough to bite through the pitted brass rail.

The Chinese man nodded to a boy in the corner who disappeared behind a dirty blue curtain that hid the deeper bowels of the hell disguised as a saloon. Within moments, the boy reappeared and behind him, the bulky form of McGee.

"Came crawling over here, didja, Addie?" He yanked up his pants with one hand and drew the other under his bulbous nose. "Brought your dogs with ya, too, eh?"

Trevor's arm tensed beneath Adelaide's. She squeezed his hand and his fingernails bit into her skin through the fabric of her sleeve. The threatening presence of Dustin remained at her left, and she heard his teeth grind together.

"I came to offer you a challenge. Winner take all—both saloons, lock, stock and barrel." As she spoke, Adelaide's voice got louder, halting any conversation in the room. "Unless of course you're too yellow."

McGee's beady eyes narrowed even further. "I ain't yellow, girlie. What challenge?"

"One game of poker, five card draw. Stakes are the saloons."

The silence in the saloon made the sound of her heart pounding seem loud. She hid her clammy palms with fisted hands. Trevor's breath hissed in and out near her ear.

McGee walked toward the bar, scratching his cheek and staring at her. Undressing her with his eyes, sending disgusted shivers of distaste down her skin. "You got balls coming in here throwing down a challenge like that. Who's gonna play for you?" He turned his gaze to Trevor. "This puppy?"

"Fuck you, McGee." Trevor's voice was low, vicious, harder than Adelaide had ever heard it before. He sounded almost like a different person.

"Now, I can have Lee here tear your man into a couple dozen pieces, Addie. Keep him on a leash or our talking is over." McGee definitely had his back up.

"Trevor will play for the Last Chance Saloon."

It was an argument Trevor knew he couldn't win, although he'd tried. He didn't want the future of her saloon in his hands, but Adelaide insisted until he gave up. She had faith in him, more faith than she thought possible. Trevor just needed to believe in himself.

"When?" McGee asked.

"Tomorrow at noon. We'll play at the Pink Kitty." Adelaide had already spoken with Maria, the madam down at the brothel, to make sure they could hold the poker game there. Maria hated McGee as much as Adelaide since he was too rough with her girls, and was happy to help.

"So we get to have a little pussy with our poker?" Laughter met McGee's crude question.

It was time for the last nail in the coffin. "We're going to put the challenge in writing with Carson."

McGee slung back the whiskey Lee had poured him, then wiped his mouth with his sleeve. "You wanna bring that lawyer in on this?"

"I want to make sure the winner gets the spoils."

The sneer in her voice made it clear she thought McGee would welch on the bet if he lost. He stepped toward her and she remained stock still, surrounded by her best friend and her lover.

When he stopped a mere inch from her, McGee's breath washed over Adelaide and she had all she could do not to gag. The man must've forgotten what tooth powder was. "You calling me a cheat?"

Someone in the saloon whistled under their breath. Adelaide refused to cower one inch from this bastard. "No, but I'm not giving you the opportunity to cheat. We play fair and square, legal before the game even begins."

Streaks of red from last night's booze surrounded the mud brown of McGee's eyes. Eyes that held not one smidge of warmth or anything good. They were cold—brought to mind the word evil, ridiculously enough. Adelaide controlled the shiver of disgust by remembering that this game would rid her of McGee one way or the other.

"Fine. Let's get Carson over here right now. I'd like to get my hands on what's in that shitty saloon of yours." His gaze dropped to her ample bosom and he licked his lips. Trevor growled behind her. "Mighty tasty treats over yonder, like that Penny gal. Oh yeah, I can think of lots of things to do in that Last Chance you got."

Adelaide nodded and waited for McGee to back up so they could leave. When he didn't, she continued to stare at him without backing up since she absolutely refused to do so.

"You're a bitch, ain't ya?"

"Count on it." Adelaide could sneer with the best of them. Life hadn't been kind to an abandoned Irish girl with a drunken grandfather and no home. There wasn't anything McGee could do to her that hadn't been done at some point in her life.

McGee finally backed off a step, far enough so Adelaide could take a breath. "Let's get to signing then, girlie. I'm itching to get winning."

A man was sent to fetch Carson Foster, who arrived at the Silver Spittoon within ten minutes, papers in hand. Adelaide had already contacted him and he was well aware of the situation. She'd only paid him to draw up the papers, nothing more. Adelaide wouldn't put it past McGee to offer him a load of money to change the wording in the agreement.

"Miss Burns, Mr. McGee," Carson said in greeting as he sat at the table. A young man with an old soul, the blond man with gray eyes had always struck her as odd. After attending college back east, when he returned to Cheyenne, he kept to himself, never showed an interest in any particular girl. Maria told her Carson visited a few of the soiled doves at the Pink Kitty so she knew he didn't prefer men. However, he didn't exactly fit in with folks in town.

Adelaide was always pleasant to him, and he was as polite as can be. It made her wonder what lay beneath the stiff lawyer exterior.

Carson laid the papers out on the scarred, dark wood table. "There are three copies here, one for each of you, and one to be filed with the magistrate. Please read them before you sign." He took out his fountain pen and waited patiently with his hands folded.

Adelaide knew what it said, but she picked up her copy and read it diligently. All laid out in neat ink, it stated that the winner of the single poker game retained the rights to the other's property, unencumbered and without prejudice. In addition, the sum of five thousand dollars would be paid to the winner and the loser would leave Cheyenne permanently.

McGee called over the boy. "Read this out loud."

The young boy took the paper with a shaking hand and a visible gulp. "Yes, Pa."

Pa? Now that was a surprise, but not really. Adelaide wasn't as much surprised to find that he had a child, but that the child was as filthy and unkempt as a street urchin. Something she was quite familiar with—no doubt the child had body lice and a layer of dirt that would take a day's soaking to get rid of.

The boy cleared his throat and started to speak, but his voice came out as a croak. McGee smacked him on the back of the head so hard he lurched forward and slammed into the table. Adelaide wanted to slap McGee until his nose met the floor, but she resisted the urge. Barely.

"Get busy, Alex." McGee didn't give the boy a moment to even catch his breath.

Alex read the paper aloud in a cracked voice, stumbling over a few of the larger words. It dawned on Adelaide that McGee probably couldn't read so he had his son do it, rather than admit he was illiterate.

After the boy finished and set the paper back on the table, he scuttled back to the corner. McGee rubbed his chin, the three-day-old whiskers rasping beneath his calloused hand. "You got yourself a deal, Addie. Mind you, if you don't hand over that saloon when I win, I claim the right to kill you."

The words sent a cold chill across her heart, but Adelaide showed no outward sign. She simply signed the three copies with a flourish and stepped back, gesturing to McGee to do the same. His signature was a shaky X and Carson witnessed both with his usual quiet demeanor.

"Thank you both. I'll leave a copy for each of you." When Carson stood to leave, his gaze locked with hers and Adelaide was surprised to see concern in his eyes. Concern for her. He seemed to be telling her to be careful. She acknowledged the silent communication and Carson did the same.

Adelaide picked up her copy of the agreement and stared hard at McGee. "Tomorrow at noon at the Pink Kitty." She waved the paper in the air. "Remember, if you don't show up, the saloon is mine by default."

"You ought to remember that yourself." McGee had threatened her and she was damn sure going to be at the Pink Kitty come hell or high water. No way was she allowing that low-down bastard to own the Last Chance.

Adelaide walked out with her head held high, Trevor and Dustin still at her side. She felt well protected. She also felt a curtain of dread fall over them which would last until noon the next day.

It was time to dance with the devil.

Brett and Noah waited for them outside the Last Chance, both armed with pistols and wearing similar menacing looks. All the men nodded to each other without speaking and Adelaide entered the saloon with four men on her tail.

"How did it go? Did he take the deal?" Brett fired questions at them.

"Not here. Let's go into the kitchen." Trevor steered Adelaide through the patrons to the back of the saloon. He wasn't surprised to find Kincaid sitting at the table in the kitchen eating a biscuit. "I figured you weren't gone yet."

Kincaid shrugged. "I was curious."

"I think you're full of shit, but I'll leave it up to Adelaide whether or not you can stay." Trevor wanted to throw the gunman out on his ass.

"Leave him be. I want to know exactly where he is until this is over." Adelaide made sense, but it didn't mean Trevor had to like it.

"The game is tomorrow at the Pink Kitty." Adelaide sat down heavily and Trevor noticed lines of stress around her eyes. "Trevor plays for the Last Chance."

Hearing it said out loud again made Trevor's stomach clench. He'd never been the one tapped for responsibility, the one everyone looked to to make everything right. It made him itch all over to even think about losing Adelaide's saloon in a game of cards.

"Are you sure you want me to play?"

Adelaide stared at him. "Yes, I'm sure. You let me know if you're not."

Well, that put it in his lap. Dammit.

Brett glanced at him, his arms folded across his chest, his gaze probing. "You've beaten everyone in Cheshire at poker. You think you can't take this fool?"

It wasn't that. Trevor knew he could play poker—hell, he'd spent the last five years honing his skills. But Adelaide taught him an important lesson when he'd lost so much to her. He'd been distracted as he expected he would be at the upcoming poker game.

"I can take him," Trevor heard himself say. His throat almost closed up and his tongue felt like a wool blanket.

Adelaide laid her hand on his arm. "Yes, you can."

ꙮ

Adelaide made Noah stay at the Last Chance with Penny and Jason while the rest of them walked over to the Pink Kitty twenty minutes before noon. They'd half-expected McGee to kill Adelaide before the game, but it didn't happen. A sleepless night and frayed tempers made for a lot of grumpy snarling, but no blows were exchanged, at least none that left any marks.

Brett stalked in front of the group, scanning the street around them, while Kincaid brought up the rear beside Dustin. Trevor kept Adelaide glued to his side. They looked like a ragtag parade walking down the wood-planked sidewalk. Folks scurried into buildings until there was no one left between them and the brothel.

Like a dime-store novel, a showdown of sorts, the entire thing felt unreal. Trevor looked so serious, Adelaide wondered if the frown marks would be permanent on his face. She tried to tease him about it, but he just ignored her.

As they walked up to the Pink Kitty's big black door, Adelaide stopped and pulled Trevor aside.

"You go in, we'll be right behind you," Adelaide said.

Brett, Kincaid and Dustin stepped back into the street and made a human wall of privacy against the town's prying gaze. She should have suspected they wouldn't listen to her. Trevor peered down at her with concern in his beautiful eyes.

"What's wrong?"

She shook her head. "Nothing's wrong. I just wanted to talk to you for a minute. Last night you all spent the entire time guarding me, I never got a chance to talk."

Adelaide stepped close and put her hand on his arm. His rigid muscles jumped beneath her fingers. "I wanted to say that it doesn't matter if you win or lose today. I trust you, Trevor. In fact...well, I don't think I can love someone, but you're sure as hell the closest I've ever been." She took a deep breath, swallowing down panic at the thought of actually confessing love to Trevor.

He cupped her cheek and slowly rubbed his thumb along her jaw. "I don't deserve your trust."

"Yes, you do." She needed for him to believe her. "You've shown me how a man can treat a woman with respect and still make her feel like a woman. You've sweated, worked and given your all to my saloon over the past month. Fact is you could've run the first night, but you never even tried. If that's not earning trust, I don't know what is."

Trevor leaned forward and kissed her on the forehead. "You make it easy to stay."

He could have told her how beautiful she was, or given some other flowery language, but he didn't. Instead he simply knocked down the wall around her heart with six words. She reached into her reticule and pulled out his marker. Without looking at his face, she ripped it into tiny pieces and let the wind steal them from her hands.

"You didn't have to do that. I owe you money."

Adelaide shook her head. "You have paid me back a thousandfold. I don't want any money from you."

"What do you want?"

"I want you to accept that your marker is gone."

He glanced at the ground as the small bits fluttered away, then back into her eyes. "I love you, Red."

"Are you ready?" She hated the huskiness in her voice almost as much as the tears pricking her eyes.

Trevor's hand dropped from her face. His demeanor grew harder in front of her eyes. "As I'll ever be."

A small crowd stood in the back of the lobby of the Pink Kitty. Normally Maria would have shooed them away, but the more people who saw the game, the better chance they had of making McGee stick to the agreement. The dark-haired madam met them at the door. She was dressed in her customary purple silk dress with her generous bosom threatening to make an appearance.

Since the older woman was a mere five feet tall, Adelaide and the group of men guarding her towered over Maria.

"Are you sure you want to do this, Adelaide?" Maria's concern was evident in her eyes, her face, even the way she clasped Adelaide's hands.

"Yes, we need to do it, Maria. You know that."

Maria nodded and glanced at the small army accompanying Adelaide. "At least I know you'll be protected." She glanced at Dustin, who actually blushed, and at Kincaid who was as expressionless as a rock. "No need to introduce myself to you." She peered at Brett and Trevor. "You two I don't know."

"Trevor Malloy, ma'am. This here's my brother, Brett." Both men tipped their hats in turn, as if they were meeting at a church social and not at a whorehouse.

"You are here to play then?" Maria's stare nearly pierced holes in Trevor.

"No, I'm here to win."

That seemed to be the right answer because Maria's expression eased and she nodded so hard the feather in her elegant coiffure bobbed dangerously. "Good, good." She turned to the boy by the door. "Alex, go to the store and get a fresh deck of cards."

After she tossed the boy a coin, McGee's son disappeared out the front door.

"McGee is in the parlor. I'm glad you are here now." Maria gestured for them to follow and the sound of the boots, the guns and the spurs on the men echoed in the small area. The scent of danger and fear glided around like an unwanted guest.

When they reached the parlor, Trevor went in first, putting Adelaide behind him. She placed her hand in the center of his back, letting him know she was there with him.

"McGee," Trevor said.

"You did show up, didja? Hm, I figured you were too yellow to even show your face after the way you were working kitchen slops."

Trevor's muscles bunched under her hand.

"Don't," Adelaide whispered.

He seemed to catch himself from lunging although a shudder ran down his body, or perhaps it was a wave of anger. It didn't matter. What mattered was that he controlled himself as she asked.

"I'll wait here," Kincaid announced as he stood on the right side of the door. One of McGee's henchmen stood on the other side. He sneered at Kincaid who simply stared at the idiot until he looked away. Kincaid nodded at her and she gently pushed Trevor into the room, followed by Brett and Dustin. Alex slid in behind them with the cards, which he handed to Maria along with the jingle of change. So the boy wasn't a thief like his father, perhaps there was hope for him.

The parlor was decorated in blues and greens, tastefully so actually. Adelaide had tea with Maria every month in the room so she knew the older woman had spent her childhood in the lap of luxury in Texas. The Pink Kitty was born of necessity and a penniless young, unmarried mother's sheer force of will.

A small round table sat in the center of the room, flanked by four fancy chairs with blue silk seats. A striped green couch was pushed against one wall with two overstuffed chairs with doilies on the arms. It was a feminine room, filled to capacity by gun-toting men.

McGee sat like a fat king at the table with his feet up and a smug grin on his face. Maria wasn't about to be cowed by him. She stomped over and shoved his feet off the table, nearly knocking him from the chair.

"You are a guest in my house. Keep your feet off the furniture," she snapped. A few snickers met her command.

"Let's get on with it then." Trevor approached the table and sat across from McGee.

Maria sat between them, the cards in front of her. She opened the box and started shuffling them with lightning-fast hands. If Trevor was surprised, he didn't show it, however McGee's eyes widened a bit. Adelaide knew Maria ten years earlier when they were both dealing cards and making a meager living at it. Their paths diverged not long after, but they had remained friends since.

"One game of five card draw, gentlemen. No wild cards, no cheating. If I think either one of you cheated, we play again. Winner takes both saloons. Are you ready?" Maria continued to shuffle the new cards, the sound of the stiff cards like an old friend to Adelaide's ears.

She grabbed Brett's arm and squeezed tightly. Everyone stood around the perimeter of the room, far enough away so the cards couldn't be seen. No one sat but the three at the table. The tension was thick and heavy, weighing on Adelaide's shoulders almost painfully. Brett didn't respond, but he covered her hand with his.

As Maria dealt the cards, time seem to slow to a crawl. Trevor picked up his hand and fanned them in front of him. Without a flicker of anything in his eyes, he glanced up at McGee, waiting. McGee chuckled and picked up his cards.

Trevor set down two cards. "I'll take two."

Adelaide noticed Maria's hands trembled slightly as she gave Trevor two cards. McGee set down one.

"And I'll take one. This is going to be too easy." He leered at Adelaide until she looked away, unwilling to show the bastard that he made her skin crawl.

Maria dealt McGee his one card then picked up the discards from the dark wood table.

"Can I make a bet on this game?" McGee asked.

Adelaide's heart pounded. "What are you talking about? There's already a bet, a mighty big one."

"I thought I'd throw in an extra five thousand dollar bet." McGee laughed and pointed at Trevor. "I hear pretty boy here likes to sell himself for it."

Trevor's hands tightened a smidge, but otherwise he didn't react. Brett spat out a curse under his breath that made Adelaide's cheeks redden.

"No changing the stakes, McGee. We're agreed and that's that." Adelaide wasn't about to let him throw anything around that might muddy the waters.

"Fine then, I guess you can't use an extra five thousand yet. Your man is going to win right?" He winked and snorted at his own wit.

"Call." Trevor's sharp voice cut through the air.

McGee raised one eyebrow. "Let's see what you've got, pretty boy. I've got three little ladies."

Three queens.

The bottom of Adelaide's stomach dropped all the way to her knees. Three of a kind was hard to beat, especially knowing that Trevor had taken two cards. He couldn't have McGee's hand beat unless a miracle happened. The Last Chance was going to be in McGee's filthy hands.

Trevor didn't blink. He glanced down at McGee's hand. "Nice. Three queens is a good hand. Too bad."

"Too bad for Addie since she'll be calling me boss." McGee stood and yanked up his pants.

"Sit down." The words shot out of Trevor's mouth and McGee sat down so fast, the chair cracked beneath him. "You haven't seen my cards yet."

Adelaide held her breath, hanging onto Brett, her link to Trevor. Against her will, hope blossomed in her chest. It was easier to recover from a blow if you were expecting it.

God, please let him win.

Trevor lay down his cards one at a time and revealed four of a kind. Deuces. All deuces. Adelaide couldn't stop the whoop that flew from her mouth. She kissed Brett on the cheek and hugged him so hard, his whiskers scraped her skin.

"He won! He won!" Adelaide smiled at Trevor and he winked. Her heart somersaulted as she realized that she was in love with him. The charming gambler who blew into her life and took more than she ever dare thought he would.

"You cheated," McGee snarled.

"I didn't cheat. I never cheat," Trevor responded in kind.

"That's a load of shit. You are a cheat."

Brett and Dustin stepped up behind Trevor. "Best be careful what you say about a Malloy," Brett said in a controlled voice.

"You lost, McGee, fair and square, with lots of witnesses. I'll give you one day to leave the Silver Spittoon before I take over." Adelaide tried not to sound smug, but it felt so good. The bastard would never go softly so she had to make sure everyone heard what he said.

"Like hell I will. We're going to play again and this time pretty boy ain't gonna cheat."

"The game was played fairly, Mr. McGee." Carson appeared from the corner of the room. "I personally witnessed the game and saw no cheating whatsoever. Under the terms of the agreement, the Silver Spittoon now belongs to Miss Burns."

McGee stood with a roar, flipping the table on its end, scattering the cards around the room. Trevor jumped back, shielding Adelaide.

"Lousy bitch and her fucking lover." McGee stalked out of the room, shoving Carson against the sofa.

Trevor turned and enfolded Adelaide in his arms. It felt so good, so right, so amazing. She tucked her head under his chin and held on tightly. They'd won. They'd actually won.

"We did it."

"No, you did it." Adelaide kissed his shoulder. "Let's go home."

Chapter Fourteen

The air in the Last Chance was celebratory. Adelaide bought a round of whiskey on the house, cheers and congratulations abounded. No one would be sorry to see McGee leave Cheyenne. Trevor sat quietly and watched Adelaide smile and relax for the first time in a week. He was happy for her, yet the shadow of McGee's threats still hung over them.

Dustin served drinks behind the bar with a scowl on his face. Not that it was unusual, but Trevor had a feeling the big man experienced the same itch of danger. Brett and Noah stood guard by the doors, checking everyone who came in.

What Trevor needed to do was figure out how to make sure McGee left town permanently. It wasn't in Trevor's nature to kill and that option would likely get his neck stretched in the process. He wasn't good at planning, that particular skill belonged to his older brother, Ray, and his brother-in-law, Tyler. He wished either one of them were there, but he refused to call for help, even if the saloon needed it.

His pride always stood in his way, but he couldn't seem to overcome it. Instead he'd protect Adelaide with his life until McGee was gone. Kincaid sat in the opposite corner, watching everyone and everything. Trevor still didn't trust that son of a bitch, but at least he hadn't done anything yet. Not that Trevor knew of anyway.

"Deep thoughts?" Kincaid's voice broke through Trevor's cloud of indecision.

"Something like that. What do you want?"

Kincaid sat down with his whiskey and propped one booted foot up on the chair. His grey eyes regarded Trevor steadily.

"You need to make sure McGee leaves Cheyenne."

Trevor wanted to punch him for even saying it out loud. "I'm not an idiot, Kincaid."

"I never said you were. Figured you were over here conjuring how to get that done."

"And you're going to help me?" That would be a bit unbelievable considering he was recently hired to kill Adelaide even if he refused the job.

"No, but I can keep an eye out, make sure he doesn't try anything."

"Don't trust him, Trevor." Brett's icy tone spoke volumes about how much he trusted the gunman.

"I wasn't planning on it, big brother."

Kincaid glanced up at Brett's stony expression. "You Malloys don't trust easy... Good." He stood and adjusted his gun belt. "Keep it that way."

Without another word, he sauntered to his perch in the back of the saloon. Brett and Trevor stared after him until they turned to look at each other.

"What do you make of him?" Brett sat down.

"I don't know what to make of him. I don't trust him, but for some stupid reason, I think he's been telling us the truth." Trevor fiddled with his empty glass.

Brett nodded. "I think he's a liar."

Trevor shrugged. "It doesn't matter. I won't trust Adelaide to him. Ever."

"So it's that way with her? You finally going to settle down?" Brett's casual words didn't match the tone of his voice.

"Why? You thinking of Adelaide for something?" Trevor's heart pounded so hard, his ears rang. Brett was smart, harder-working and more stable than Trevor would ever be. Adelaide would be getting a good catch if she snagged Brett.

Of course, Trevor would have to leave Wyoming if that happened.

"Not really. Just curious." Brett's eyes never revealed what he was thinking, damn him. Trevor had the urge to use a stick to open up Brett's brain just to find out what was in his head.

"She's mine."

Even if she didn't know it yet.

Hours later, the saloon quieted down, then closed for the night. Trevor waited until Adelaide was ready to escort her upstairs. Dustin, Brett and Noah worked out a schedule to be on guard in four-hour shifts through the following morning. No one was taking any chances. Kincaid had disappeared in the crowd and Trevor hadn't spotted his dark head again. That didn't mean he was gone for good so he was another threat to be on the lookout for.

"Thank you," Adelaide said as they walked up the stairs.

"For what?"

"For winning that game. I was prepared to lose...well, not really, but I'm so glad you won. I didn't want to leave Cheyenne." She stopped at her doorway. "And I didn't want to leave you."

Trevor's mouth dropped open and he stood like a statue in the hallway until she realized he hadn't followed her in. She cocked her head and the corners of her mouth tilted in the smallest, sexiest of grins.

"You coming, cowboy?"

As Trevor stepped toward her, time seemed to slow to a crawl. Her expression of sweet seduction turned into one of anger and fear. She ran toward him with a shout.

Her shoulder slammed into his stomach so hard, it stole his breath. The sound of a gunshot split the air followed by the shattering of the mirror behind him. Trevor started falling toward the floor as a second gunshot rang out. He felt a sting on his shoulder and felt Adelaide jerk on top of him as they hit the floor.

"Son of a bitch!" Brett shouted as he ran past the door in a blur. Following him was Noah and somehow, Kincaid. Dustin appeared in the doorway and his normally ruddy face blanched when he looked at Adelaide and Trevor in a heap on the floor.

"Sweet Jesus," the big man said under his breath. "Adelaide."

Trevor realized that Adelaide wasn't moving and he was still so winded, he couldn't even reach for her. He pleaded with his eyes for Dustin to help.

Dustin shouted for Marybeth loud enough to make the walls shake, then he knelt down and gently lifted Adelaide off Trevor. A drop of warmth landed on Trevor's cheek. It took him a moment or two to realize it wasn't tears.

It was blood.

Adelaide's blood.

Trevor's vision started to blur as he rolled over on his side, desperately trying to get a breath in. A swift smack landed square on his back and he inhaled sharply, the much-needed air burning his lungs. Marybeth hovered above him. Damn she had a hard hand.

"You okay, Trevor?" Marybeth asked.

He nodded and she headed for Adelaide's bed. Trevor got up on all fours and took two deep breaths, ignoring the pain in his shoulder. When he finally made it to his feet, the world tilted a bit. He stumbled toward Adelaide, trying not to think of all the reasons why she would be bleeding on him.

"Looks like it hit her right above the heart. Clean shot too, went right through her," Marybeth said in a low voice.

Shot? She'd been shot?

"Yep, and I think I know where the bullet is too." Dustin's voice echoed through Trevor's ears.

Trevor glanced down and realized the front of his shirt was covered with blood. Hers. And his.

"You gonna faint?" Dustin growled.

"No, don't think so." Everything was so wrong, so unreal. Trevor sat on the edge of the bed, staring at the pale, bleeding woman who apparently threw herself in front of a bullet for him.

She'd risked her life. Perhaps even given her life.

For him. Trevor Malloy, the silver-tongued gambler with shit for brains.

"Oh, damn, he said he wasn't going to faint," Dustin said as Trevor felt himself falling toward the floor again.

ℵ

Trevor awoke in his room to lamplight and hushed voices somewhere in the distance. His left shoulder felt tight and sore, and when he went to shift positions, he realized it was bandaged as well.

Everything hit him at once.

Adelaide shot, the blood, the agony of knowing what she'd done for him. A sob crept up his throat and he swallowed it back through sheer force of will. He had to find out if she was alive or not.

Then he'd kill the bastard who shot her.

"You awake?" Brett's voice came from across the room in the shadows.

"Sorta. Feel like I've been kicked by a bronc."

Brett walked toward the bed, a dark figure in the gloom. "Nope, just a Colt Peacemaker. Son of a bitch ran like the wind too. We didn't catch him." When he stepped into the lamplight, Trevor was surprised to see so much concern on Brett's face.

"Was I that bad off?" Trevor joked weakly, knowing Brett's concern wasn't solely for him, dreading the response.

"No, and you know that. You conked your head on the door and had a minor gunshot wound. Marybeth fixed you up quick. It's Adelaide you should be worried about." Brett's normally stern expression became grave. "She hasn't woken up yet since the doc finished with her. Had to do a lot of stitching to close her up after that bullet ripped through her."

Trevor's eyes pricked with tears and his throat closed so tight, he knew he couldn't speak. Instead he focused on breathing in and out, not thinking about his beautiful Red lying half-dead in the room next door. Not thinking about the fact that she might die and leave him alone.

Not after he'd just found her after a lifetime of searching.

Brett seemed to understand that Trevor needed time to compose himself. He stood patiently, staring off through the window into the darkened night. When Trevor cleared his throat for the third time, he finally formed the words he'd wanted to blurt.

"Will she die?"

No, please say no.

"The doc says he isn't sure. She lost a lot of blood, but she's strong, a fighter. A fever hasn't taken hold yet so that's good. But she is in what they call a coma, like a deep sleep where nothing gets to her."

Trevor didn't think Brett had given him all the details, but he didn't push for more. In fact, what Trevor needed was to touch her.

Right now.

He rose from the bed shirtless, glad to have his britches on at least, and stumbled toward the door, the cool wood a relief beneath his bare feet. Brett caught his arm.

"Whoa, where you going?"

"Do you really need to ask me that question?" Trevor shrugged off Brett's hold and concentrated on walking toward the door. By the time he reached it, the dizziness had nearly passed. What he wanted to do was run, but what he could do was go slowly into the hallway and to Adelaide's room.

Her door stood ajar, a peep of light streaming into the hallway. Trevor's mouth went cotton dry as he pushed the door open and entered. Marybeth sat on a chair next to the bed with some knitting in her hands. It registered that Trevor never knew she knitted before his thoughts moved past her and onto the bed.

Adelaide looked like a red-haired angel enveloped in white. White sheets, white bandages, white nightdress. Her normally pink complexion appeared as pale as the linens surrounding her.

"She's been calling for you."

Trevor didn't remember approaching the bed, but he found himself on his knees with Adelaide's hand pressed against his cheek while he cried silently. Huge wet tears of regret splashed onto his hands and chest.

"Oh, Red, why did you do it?" he mumbled as he kissed her hand. "You can't die because of me."

The door shut quietly and Trevor realized Marybeth had left the room. Trevor climbed onto the bed, careful not to disturb Adelaide, and got as close as he could. The heat from her body mixed with his and the absolute terror inside him subsided. He breathed in her scent, and prayed to God to spare Adelaide and take him, until sleep claimed him.

ꕥ

"You can't go anywhere."

"Like hell I can't. Tyler showed up with his two marshal friends and we're going after that son of a bitch." Trevor continued to stuff his belongings into the saddlebags that had lain empty for over a month.

Brett glowered, his hands on his hips. "You're just going to leave the woman you love in a coma to go chasing after a piece of shit like McGee?"

"You know as well as I do that he's the one who hired someone to kill me. She was the one who took the bullet with my name on it. I'm going to make that bastard pay one way or the other." Trevor had waited three days, three excruciating days until his brother-in-law, Tyler, arrived. An ex-bounty hunter and the biggest, meanest son of a bitch Trevor knew, Tyler could track anyone and anything. He had to help find

McGee. Trevor slung his saddle bags up on his good shoulder and headed out of the room.

"What happens if she wakes up?" Brett blocked the door.

"Stay here and guard her, Brett. When she wakes up tell her I'm sorry, that I love her, and that I never meant for her to give her life for mine. I'm not worth it." Trevor's voice broke on the last word but he refused to shed one more tear. He'd cried an ocean the last two days and finally remembered that he was a man. Men didn't sit on their asses and wait for justice to happen. Men served justice.

"Coward."

Brett's vehemence nearly gave Trevor pause. His brother was right—he was a coward. Running because he couldn't watch Adelaide die a little bit more each day, her skin so pale the veins shone blue through her cheeks. It was slowly killing him and he just couldn't sit there and do nothing anymore.

Perhaps it was the coward's way to leave her to other's care, but Trevor didn't know what else to do besides go insane. He served no purpose other than to sit by the bed and watch. He acquired a mission—to find McGee and he was damn sure going to follow through with it.

He stomped down the stairs with Brett hot on his heels. Dustin guarded the door, arms folded across his massive chest. Tyler stood beside him, his cool blue eyes piercing in the morning light. Over six feet tall, and two hundred twenty pounds, Tyler Calhoun was Noah's adopted father and husband to the only Malloy sister, Nicky. Tyler was hands down the fastest, smartest bounty hunter who ever came out of Texas, and he appreciated the fact that family helped each other whenever and wherever. Retired for the last six years, Tyler still retained all his instincts and skills. He needed them being married to an ornery woman like Nicky.

Family was why Tyler came when Trevor called, and brought the marshals with him to apprehend McGee, now an outlaw wanted for attempted murder and arson. He'd apparently lit the Silver Spittoon on fire before leaving town. Luckily the fire had been put out before any extensive damage happened. He'd kept the fire brigade busy the last month. If he ever stepped foot in Cheyenne again, no doubt they'd string him up without a trial.

"Trevor, you don't have to come," Tyler's deep voice warned him.

"Yes, I do. I can't sit up there day after day and watch her die. Don't tell me I can't come, Tyler, or I'll dog you anyway." Trevor shook with the need to simply get on his horse and ride.

Tyler nodded. "I figured as much. I thought I'd point out Nicky would likely blister your ass for joining a posse three days after getting shot."

"She's not here to do it so I'm not too worried about it. You gonna let me ride with you, Tyler?" Trevor snapped.

"I don't have much of a choice, do I?" He jerked his thumb toward Dustin. "This man here might have a say in it though."

"Do you think I shouldn't go?" Trevor challenged.

Dustin stared at him with his dark eyes, full of a myriad of emotions, not the least of which was boiling anger. "One of us has to stay here. I figure I'd need to break your leg to make you stay."

Trevor knew by Dustin's tone that he'd contemplated doing just that. "I appreciate your restraint, Dustin."

Dustin snorted. "You make sure you come back here, pretty boy. If you don't, I'll find you."

The threat was clear and Trevor understood why. If, no *when* Adelaide woke up, she'd want to know where Trevor was.

They'd been stuck like two peas in a pod for over a month, and more than half of that in bed together. Trevor wouldn't simply abandon her.

"I'll be back, even if it's belly down on a horse." Trevor knew the danger was very real, so was the possibility that he could be killed.

"Just so we're agreed on that." Dustin stepped aside and Trevor had the feeling he'd just escaped a beating.

Trevor spotted Noah standing in the shadows by the door. The young man scowled blackly at his father. No doubt he had received the tongue-lashing of his life for leaving home without letting Tyler know about it.

"Noah's headed home." Tyler shot a glance at Noah. "Isn't that right?"

Noah grunted and shoved off the wall. "I'd rather ride with you, Pa."

"I know that and we've been through it at least ten times. You are foreman on my ranch, which means your ass belongs back there, not joining a posse," Tyler said tightly.

"Still don't like it," Noah mumbled.

"That's just tough shit. Next time don't leave home without telling me." He held up his hand to forestall the argument about to burst from Noah's mouth. "I don't care if your ma knew or not, *I* didn't know."

"Fine then. I'm going home after you leave."

"No, you're going now. That lady in the kitchen even fixed you some vittles to take with you, even if it's only a few hours. Pick up your pack and go." Tyler stepped toward Noah when he didn't move.

To his credit, Noah didn't flinch. He simply picked up the burlap sack from the table next to him, nodded at everyone and silently walked out.

That boy was definitely on his way to becoming a man. Trevor shifted the saddlebags on his shoulders. A twinge in his shoulder constantly reminded him of the reason he was leaving. To find Adelaide's would-be murderer and bring him to justice. Tyler followed Trevor out the door and into the crisp spring air. Time to go hunting.

Chapter Fifteen

Adelaide swam in an ocean of pain and confusion. Sounds, voices and the constant throb in her chest reminded her that she was still alive. She surely hadn't landed in heaven, or there wouldn't be so much pain. She recognized Marybeth's voice, and Dustin's, and another strange man. One voice reminded her of Trevor, but it wasn't quite him, perhaps Brett.

She swam through the fog surrounding her, desperate to break the surface and into the light again. The darkness weighed heavily on her, sometimes she just cried for the absoluteness of it.

"You're restless tonight, Adelaide," Marybeth said. "Maybe some laudanum would help."

No!

Adelaide wanted to shout, but all she did was moan loudly and flap her left hand. A pause and then Marybeth spoke directly in her ear. "Adelaide?"

Adelaide tried again to speak, but her mouth seemed to have forgotten how to work. Tears leaked down her cheeks when all she could do was moan again.

"You can hear me, can't you?"

This time Adelaide was able to nod.

"Holy Mary, you're awake!" Marybeth kissed her soundly on the forehead. "Oh, sweetie, don't cry."

Marybeth dabbed at her face with a handkerchief, which just made Adelaide cry harder. The fortunate side effect of the tears was that her eyes grew moistened enough to open a peek. The glare from the lamplight stung and she blinked rapidly to lessen the pain.

"Trevor," Adelaide managed to mumble, or tried to anyway.

Marybeth laid her hand on Adelaide's forehead and sighed. "He's gone after that lowdown snake McGee. Foolish man lit his own saloon on fire before he hightailed it out of town. Trevor called in his brother-in-law and some marshals and took off after McGee. What with the gunshot wound, I tried to talk—"

Adelaide started choking when she tried to speak. Gunshot wound? Trevor had been shot?

Marybeth cupped the back of her neck and brought a cup of water to Adelaide's mouth. "Drink, then talk. It's been a week, and your throat is likely not working right yet."

After the cool liquid slid down her throat, Adelaide was able to speak again. "Who shot Trevor?"

Marybeth cocked her head. "Why the same bullet that went through you went into him. You saved his life, Adelaide."

Adelaide remembered in a flash. The shadow in the hallway outside her room, the glint of the barrel aimed at Trevor's back. She had tried to knock him out of the way, followed by searing pain and then nothing.

"When will he be back?" Adelaide desperately needed to see him, touch him, feel him.

Marybeth's expression became evasive. "I don't rightly know, Adelaide. He didn't say for sure."

Along with the pain from the gunshot wound came the agony of knowing Trevor had chosen revenge over her. Even if he did it in her name, he'd left her unconscious to pursue a vendetta. Adelaide's tears fell for quite some time.

ꝏ

A week later, Adelaide awoke to find Dustin sleeping in a chair next to her bed. Sore, unhappy and itchy, she still found a smile when she noticed how uncomfortable he looked. Neck bent to one side, mouth open, snoring to wake the dead. He had stubble on his chin, and his clothes definitely needed a good washing.

"You here to serve me breakfast, big man?"

Adelaide's voice startled him and he nearly fell off the chair. Arms flailing, he righted himself before disaster struck. She hadn't meant to scare him, but it just made the sight of him that much funnier. As laughter struck, so did more pain, the muscles in her chest screeched in protest. She wheezed and clutched her arm to her chest.

Dustin jumped up and raced to her side, worry plain in his eyes. "Adelaide, you okay?"

"Yes." She bit her lip to keep the tears from flowing. She'd cried enough tears in the last week to fill an ocean. No more needed to fall. After a few minutes of Dustin hovering over her, she waved him away and sat up slowly. The pain receded to a dull roar, enough that she could at least speak again.

"Can you get me some tea?"

He nodded and left the room without a word. The sounds of morning in the saloon drifted through the open door. She heard Marybeth and Dustin, then the quieter voice of Penny. Dishes rattled and a few curses flew. Motley as they were, the folks in the Last Chance were her family and she loved them.

The last week had taught her another important lesson. She loved Trevor. Loved him with everything she had, dammit. A million times a day she wondered if he'd come back. Two million times a day she reminded herself it didn't matter.

Of course that was a bald-faced lie. She wanted him to come back so badly, just so she could tell him she loved him. He'd told her, but Adelaide never had the courage to say it back to him. Probably because she hadn't wanted to admit it to herself.

"Adelaide?" The voice at the door sounded so much like Trevor, her stomach fluttered and her eyes pricked with longing. But it wasn't Trevor—it was Brett.

"Come on in. I'm as decent as I'm going to get." Adelaide waved him in.

Brett walked like a cat, deliberate and methodical, putting each foot in a particular spot before stepping forward. He exuded an air of aloofness, someone who preferred his own company to others. Adelaide wasn't quite sure what to make of him, so she watched him a lot. He also had excellent observation skills because he'd caught her watching him more than once. His eyes revealed nothing of what he was thinking.

"Mornin'." His usual greeting.

"Good morning, Brett." Adelaide indicated the chair recently vacated by her sleeping protector. "Sit, please."

He sat down carefully, perched on the seat like a gentleman at a fancy ball. Brett Malloy was all about manners and appearances. Adelaide kind of liked that about him.

"How are you feeling?" The same words he'd spoken yesterday and the day before.

"I'm better every day. I told you that there was no need for you to stay here any longer. Don't they need you at home?" She felt more than a bit of guilt that Brett hung around protecting her from a threat that was likely halfway to Mexico.

"It's my duty to stay here until everything is settled."

Now that was a cryptic response. "What does that mean?"

Brett cut his gaze to the window. "A Malloy is a Malloy for life. One for all and all for one, like the musketeers. It's my duty to stay."

"Until when?"

"Until Trevor comes back. Or Tyler does."

This time Brett's response struck a chord. "Do you mean Trevor might never come back? Or that he might not be able to?"

"Doesn't matter one way or the other. Once the business is taken care of with McGee, I'll go home." Brett's stony expression still told her nothing.

"It matters to me! I care if Trevor comes back or not."

"So do I," Brett said quietly. It was the first time Adelaide had seen some emotion from the taciturn man. Concern flashed through his eyes. "I've got to keep watch. Since Jack, Ray and Ethan can't be here, then it's me."

"Would they all come if they could?" It seemed impossible to her.

"Yes, of course."

Another straight, flat answer.

"And you always help each other, no matter what?"

"No matter what."

The very idea fascinated Adelaide, a girl who grew up under the shadow of her drunken grandfather. Family meant nothing more than the folks you shared a cheap room with. Apparently to the Malloys, it meant everything.

"That means you're my shadow then?"

"I reckon so." Brett stood. "I'm going to go back to my post now."

His post was a chair outside Adelaide's room that he occupied most hours of the day, unless someone else relieved him. Brett was nothing if not diligent and hard-working, unlike his free-spirited brother.

Of course, Brett never smiled or cracked a joke, or even relaxed for a moment. That wasn't normal in Adelaide's opinion. Actually what she really thought was that Brett needed a woman. Too bad Penny didn't like him. As it was, every time Adelaide saw her, Penny was moping, missing Noah. Her long face was about to drive Adelaide crazy every time she poked her head in to say hello.

Adelaide couldn't count the number of times Penny had asked if Noah was coming back. She obviously missed her chosen man.

Just as Adelaide did.

Where was Trevor?

ജര

In a small valley in northwest Texas, Trevor took a swig from the water skin on his shoulder. Damn, it was hot in Texas, especially in July. The sun beat down like a frying pan on his head, then it was dark as pitch at night. Tyler had tracked McGee to a bandito hideout in the hills, then the posse camped behind some rocks and waited.

Trevor was sick of waiting and made sure he let Tyler know. Now he had one annoyed ex-bounty hunter and two suffering marshals ready to wring his neck. They sat around a cold fire, gnawing on some jerky and staring holes into each other.

"So what are we waiting for?" Tyler asked for the tenth time that day.

Tyler shifted his gaze to Trevor's and he frowned. "A little help. I'm not going into another bandito hideout alone."

Trevor sighed, missing Adelaide, wondering if she was alive. No, no, no. She definitely lived—he'd know it in his chest, in his heart, if she didn't. He wondered if Marybeth was making biscuits that morning, or if Dustin had restocked the liquor from the supply that had come in the day before Trevor left.

Startled, Trevor realized that he'd made a life with Adelaide and everyone else at the Last Chance. He'd found a place where he belonged, where he felt needed and where he loved. What was he doing chasing after McGee? That was a lawman's job, not a saloon sweep's.

Adelaide.

He could picture her sweet red curls, her bountiful breasts and the delicious curve of her hip. God he hoped she was okay. The first town they got to, he'd send a telegram and tell her he loved her. He didn't care if half the town read it. He wanted her to know.

The cold nose of a pistol pressed against the back of his ear.

"*Hola, gringo.* You waiting for someone, no?" a man whispered.

"Malcolm?"

"Trevor?"

Trevor whirled around to find Malcolm Ross, the bandito formerly known as Hermano, and honorary member of the Malloy clan. A half-Spaniard, half-Scotsman who always dressed in dark colors, Malcolm lived on a ranch in southeastern Texas with his wife Leigh. He and Tyler had never been anything more than civil enemies, but Trevor always liked Malcolm, even when he lived as Hermano.

A handshake turned into a hug as they were surrounded by Tyler, the marshals and a few of Malcolm's men.

"*Gringo.*" Malcolm nodded at Tyler.

"Nice of you to finally show up," Tyler snapped.

Malcolm raised one eyebrow. "It's good to see you, too. How is Roja and the *hijos*?"

"Nicky's fine and so are the young'uns. Now, will you help us get that fat little bastard out of that hideout or am I wasting my time?" It wasn't in Tyler's nature to be anything but blunt, with an edge.

Malcolm smiled. "You will never change, eh, *gringo*? *Si*, I will help get you in. You must not speak a word, but pretend to be my cousin, Luis. The rest of you must stay here. I will take Diego and Ramon with me for protection."

Trevor really wanted to be the one to go into the hideout, but with his reddish-brown hair he'd stand out like a whore in church. His palms itched to do something other than wait, dammit. Adelaide was his to protect, his to avenge. A surge of resentment washed through him as he watched as the small pack of banditos mounted their horses and turned toward the valley behind them.

"You keep watch, Trevor. Stay with Bill and Hector." Tyler treated him as if he were a child.

That was the straw that broke the camel's back, so to speak. Trevor's mind was made up and he'd not stay behind.

"I'm not a fifteen-year-old boy, Tyler. I've survived thirty-two years on this earth without you telling me where to piss. I will not stay here while you go after the man who tried to kill me and my woman. This is *my* fight." Trevor prepared to get the crap kicked out of himself if necessary, but he was going.

"You don't look like a bandito, Trevor," Malcolm remarked.

"So I'll smear shit in my hair and dirt on my face and rip my clothes," Trevor snapped.

Malcolm chuckled. "You are determined then. Do you at least speak Spanish, *amigo*?"

Trevor forced himself not to snap again. "I can get by."

"You're not a gunslinger, Trevor." Tyler frowned. "This isn't a fight in a saloon anymore. The men in that bandito hideout would rather slit your throat than talk to you. It ain't gonna be easy and it sure as hell ain't gonna be fun."

"I'm going." Trevor didn't care about the danger. A man possessed, Trevor absolutely had to confront McGee, to get retribution for what was done to the woman he loved.

"So be it. You listen to me, do as I say, no matter what. *Comprende*?" Malcolm's face hardened into a mask of cool menace, no doubt what he wore when he rode as the bandito Hermano for fifteen years.

"I got it. Let's go get that piece of shit." Trevor tightened his gun belt.

"Let us get you and the *gringo* ready." Malcolm shot a sidelong glance at Tyler and grinned. "We're going to need some dirt."

It took them about ten minutes to coat Trevor's hair with enough dirt that it looked dark brown, and his skin to look dirty enough to pass as half-white. Trevor spit out the dirt that got into his mouth to the raucous laughter of Malcolm and his friends.

With that, the five men rode off into the afternoon sun, into the realm of outlaws, a world completely unknown to Trevor. Malcolm, Diego and Ramon sat back comfortably in their saddles, but their pistols rested in their hands. Tyler simply glared, as was his usual way of things, and that made him intimidating enough that no one would bother him. Although his size usually accomplished that.

Trevor decided to be the quiet, brooding one. He'd watched Brett his whole life, he should be able to mimic his brother's intensity. As they rode into the narrow canyon, the sound of a rifle cocking stopped them in their tracks. The dry dirt created a cloud of dust around them from the horses' hooves.

"*¿Quien es?*" a man asked from above.

"*Soy Hermano y mis amigos. Necessitamos agua,*" Malcolm called back.

"Hermano? What do you mean? He's been dead five years." A second rifle cocked.

A trickle of sweat ran down the center of Trevor's back. He tried to swallow but his throat was as dry as the ground around him, not to mention the aftertaste of his dirt bath. His hat shaded the sun somewhat, but he dared not look up at the voice for fear his anxiousness would make him stupid. God knows, he didn't need help being stupid.

"*Si*, I am Hermano." Malcolm took off his hat and spread his arms wide. "I am not dead, *amigo.*"

A few moments later, Trevor heard the scrape of a boot as someone climbed down the rock face. A short swarthy man appeared with a pair of pistols pointed at them. His dark eyes shone as cold as the fear spreading through Trevor.

"Santiago?" Malcolm asked.

"Hermano?" The man peered at Malcolm more closely. "It is you. *Bienvenido!*"

Thank God Tyler had called Malcolm and asked him to help. They never would have made it into the bandito hideout without him. Well, Tyler might have made it in by killing everyone he saw, but that wasn't the best way to do it.

The five of them rode in to find a cluster of crude dwellings, mostly made with sticks, straw, some Mexican serapes, and what smelled like dried mud. Several fires burned with men clustered around them, darkened shadows in the gathering dusk. A breeze blew against Trevor's face and he had to force himself to resist the urge to shudder. This place smelled of danger and one wrong move could put him in a shallow grave on a west Texas hill.

A few folks stared at them as they passed. Malcolm acknowledged those he knew, ignored the others. They approached the biggest fire and Malcolm dismounted, gesturing for the rest of them to do the same. As Trevor's feet hit the ground, he felt the full impact of at least fifty people staring at him in and around the hideout. It didn't matter how scared he was, his mission was to find McGee and he didn't care how he accomplished it.

A tall, thin man with a scar bisecting his face, who hadn't seen a bar of soap in probably two years, stood smoking a cigarillo by the fire. Obviously a man of stature, as it were, in the bandito community, his gaze locked on Malcolm.

"*¿Hermano, como esta?*" he asked. He took a drag off the cigarillo.

"I live, Jose. I have new *amigos* that ride with me. We are on our way to Mexico and our canteens went dry."

Thank God Malcolm had the foresight to dump their water before they left camp. Trevor had been too worked up to even think of an excuse to get into the hideout.

Jose grunted. "*Si*, you can help yourself to water... Why are you really here, Hermano?"

Malcolm laughed. "You are too smart. I look for a man that shot a woman in the back. I need to teach him a lesson."

"Ah, I see. You think this man is here?" Jose glanced around. "In this valley?"

"*Si*, I hear things," was all Malcolm said.

"*¿Qué es su nombre?*"

Malcolm stepped over to the fire, out of range for Trevor to hear. As Malcolm spoke to Jose, Trevor leaned a little closer to Tyler.

"What's he doing?" Trevor hissed.

"Shut up, fool," Tyler said without moving his lips.

Dammit to hell. Trevor hated not knowing what Malcolm was doing and he hated being afraid. The need for revenge was stronger than his fear, but they were both making him crazy. He hoped this Jose would help them find McGee so they could get the hell out of there.

Malcolm walked back toward them and mounted his horse. "Let's go, *amigos*."

Trevor stared at him openmouthed. What the hell? That was it?

"I said, let's go," Malcolm said in a low, sharp voice.

Tyler wasn't as subtle. "*Vamanos, estúpido.*"

With words crowding in his mouth, Trevor allowed his common sense to take hold of his anger and he jumped on Silver. They'd come all that way to leave empty-handed? Wasn't McGee there at the hideout?

They rode toward the edge of the buildings, then Malcolm stopped. "We wait here."

"Wait for—"

"Shut up," Malcolm snapped.

Trevor shut up, but he wasn't happy about shutting up. A few minutes passed by with only the swishing of the horses' tails and the lengthening of the shadows. He controlled the impulse to force Malcolm to tell him what was going on, but just barely.

Jose appeared on a horse and rode up to them. "The man you seek is in the second hut beneath the canyon rim." He pointed to a hut about three hundred yards away. "The gringo had lots of money and liquor so we let him stay. If he shoots *mujeres* in the back then he deserves whatever you give him. *Adios*, Hermano." He disappeared back into the lair from which he'd come.

Trevor stared at the hut, at the bright red, orange and black serape that hung as a door. His heart thumped painfully. He hadn't been sure if the courage existed within him to kill a man. All he had to do was remember Adelaide lying helpless on the bed, swathed in white, and the fury that overtook him gave him all the courage he needed.

"He's mine."

No one argued, no one even said a word. Using hand signals, Malcolm sent Diego and Ramon on the right side, and took a scowling Tyler on the left. Trevor headed straight for the door. When he arrived, he heard the tinkling of broken glass, and a man's curse.

"Stupid whore! Just suck it! What are ya, a retard?"

Seconds later, a half-dressed young woman burst from the hut and stopped dead in front of Trevor. With eyes that reflected a lifetime of enduring men like McGee, she glanced at Trevor's pistols then nodded. Like a wisp of smoke, she was gone.

Trevor dismounted and took a deep, steadying breath. As he approached the hut, the serape was thrown back and McGee stumbled out. The last three weeks had not been kind to the rotund Irishman. He hadn't shaved, nor washed, since he'd escaped Cheyenne. His clothes were nowhere to be seen, instead he wore a union suit covered with various stains of questionable origins.

"Maria, or Anita, whatever the hell your name is, you come back here!" McGee hadn't even noticed Trevor.

"McGee." Trevor's voice trembled with rage. Rage for every drop of blood that had been stolen from Adelaide, for every moment of pain she suffered, and for every second of her life she'd lost.

"Heh? Who is that?" McGee peered at Trevor with bloodshot eyes. "Is that the pretty cowboy? What the fuck are you doing here?"

"Hunting."

That one word sent McGee scrambling back into the hut more quickly than Trevor thought he could move. Trevor ran after him, entering the musty, dark hut with his pistol drawn. The flash of a gun allowed him to see where McGee sat on the floor.

He pointed his pistol and fired, ignoring the sting on his cheek and the pain in his thigh. He fired until there were no bullets left in his gun. Until Tyler pushed his hands down.

"It's over, Trevor."

Trevor felt like a man in a trance. Someone led him outside where he leaned his forehead against Silver's neck and tried to suck in much-needed air. He'd killed a man. It had been a fair fight to be sure, but just the same, Trevor had killed a man.

And he was glad of it. Now, he could go home.

Malcolm came up next to him. "The *bandejo* won't be bothering your woman anymore, Trevor."

Trevor glanced at the ex-bandito. "Thank you for everything. I...I couldn't have found him or gotten to him without you and your friends."

"I owe your family much I can never repay. This was easy." Malcolm grinned and touched his finger to his flat-brimmed hat. "I'm on my way back home to Leigh."

A few more farewells and Malcolm rode off with his quiet friends.

"What do we do with the body?" Trevor figured McGee's body would be putting off a stench in no time, especially in mid-summer.

"Bill and Hector will take him in to the closest sheriff. And we can go home."

Tyler's words echoed through Trevor's head. After weeks of doing nothing but sitting on his ass to seek revenge against a man, suddenly it was all over in an instant.

Home. Time to return to Adelaide.

ฆ๑ઉ

Adelaide figured she wouldn't get many more surprises, but she was wrong. Three weeks after the shooting, Dustin came in with lunch, followed by Marybeth. Adelaide was ready to start walking again, but the two of them had conspired to keep her bed bound.

Marybeth carried a sandwich and Dustin a jar of water and a pickle. The twin expressions on their faces sent a shiver of dread up her spine.

"What is it? Did you hear from Trevor?"

The two of them exchanged glances then turned back to Adelaide.

"What? What is it? Don't make me get out of this bed and kick your ass, Dustin." Adelaide's anger mixed with fear, a dangerous combination.

"We got a telegram from Tyler, Trevor's brother-in-law," Dustin said quietly.

The bell of doom clanged in Adelaide's head. That couldn't be good news.

"Dustin," she growled.

Marybeth sat on the edge of the bed, her chocolate eyes brimming with concern. "He said McGee was dead in a shoot-out in a bandito hideout, but he didn't say anything about Trevor. Not a word."

What did it mean? That Trevor was killed in the shoot-out too? Or wounded again?

"Did you send a response?"

"It was too late. Marvin took his sweet time bringing the telegram over, sanctimonious ass. By the time we got it, a day had passed. I'm sure Tyler is long gone from the town he wired from." Marybeth sighed heavily.

"Did you try?"

"Yes, honey, we did, but they didn't get it. He said he'd stop in Grayton so I'll send a wire there for him to pick up." Dustin sat on the other side. Adelaide suddenly felt like these two people, a mismatched pair of guardian angels, were like the parents she'd never had. A mother and father who were concerned about her, showed her love, care and everything real parents should. Her throat closed up and tears flooded her eyes. Goddamn watering pot.

"Thank you for telling me. Did Tyler say where they were?"

"Somewhere in west Texas in the hills. I expect it will be another two weeks or more before they make it back." Marybeth handed her the sandwich. "Now you need to eat if you want to try and walk today."

Adelaide took the sandwich dutifully and Dustin put the water on the stand next to the bed.

"Thank you. Both of you..." Adelaide swallowed the lump in her throat. "I love you."

The comical expressions on their faces would forever stay in Adelaide's memory. Dustin looked panicked while Marybeth looked like she'd been slapped.

"I don't mean I'm in love with you, just that...you're my family and I love you," Adelaide explained further.

Dustin dropped a quick kiss on her forehead, patted her shoulder and darted from the room. Marybeth clasped her hands in front of her like a woman in prayer. When she looked up at Adelaide, a single tear streaked down her rounded cheek.

"I love you too, Adelaide. The daughter I could never have."

Adelaide's chest filled with the breath of life and she hugged her dear friend. Lucky to have a family who loved her. Hoping life would give her more of it.

Soon.

Chapter Sixteen

About two days after they headed back to Wyoming, Trevor figured out Tyler was teaching him a lesson. A hard lesson in not leaving a woman to go chasing outlaws. Tyler sent a telegram to Adelaide letting her know that McGee was dead and that they were on their way back. Then they hightailed it out of town before a response came back to let them know how Adelaide was.

Trevor had a graze on his cheek from McGee's wild shots, and Tyler had dug a bullet out of Trevor's thigh, which hurt like hell, but it was nothing compared to the pain in his heart. Trevor was nearly plum crazy worrying about her, whether or not she woke up or if she was in pain. He missed her like hell and couldn't wait to get back to Cheyenne.

And grovel.

Something he wanted to do by telegram, if at all possible. God knows he didn't want to get down on his knees in front of her. Damn Tyler wouldn't let Trevor go near a town, nor would he tell him exactly what else was in the telegram that he'd sent. He hadn't let Trevor see it, in fact, he wouldn't let him in the telegram office. All Tyler did say was that he had a horse auction he had to get back for so they were riding like demons back home. That fact didn't bother Trevor much—he wanted to get back quickly for his own reasons. The two marshals split off on their own way with McGee's body so that left Trevor and Tyler traveling alone.

Lucky, lucky, lucky.

If there was ever a less fun traveling partner than Tyler Calhoun, Trevor would be incredibly surprised. Tyler was as talkative as Brett, meaning, not at all. He also grumped and growled a lot, like Ray. He ate like a bear too, like Noah.

Tyler was a mixture of all the various odd or annoying parts of the Malloy family.

Oh yes, lucky indeed.

Their conversation over breakfast was as boring as the conversation over the noon meal, and was repeated again over supper. Five days of non-conversation had Trevor ready to sit on his brother-in-law and make him talk.

Fortunately for Trevor's sanity, they were getting closer to Cheyenne. Only nine days out if his memory served him right. Thank God and all the heavenly saints. It was a cool morning, but the sun was already burning off the dew, creating little wisps of steam on the prairie grass. The horses grazed nearby, munching on the sweet wet breakfast.

Tyler built up the fire to make coffee while Trevor made pan biscuits. Not as good as his mother's or his sister-in-law Lily's, but edible at least.

"You plan on marrying her when you get back?" Tyler's question nearly knocked Trevor on his ass. It was the most words Tyler had strung together the entire ride home.

"Are you talking to me?" Trevor couldn't help himself.

"Don't make me hurt you, Trevor," Tyler warned with a hint of retribution in his eyes. "Just answer the question. You gonna marry that gal or not?"

"Since you haven't once asked me about Adelaide, or would even let me send her a telegram, I find it hard to believe you're interested in what I'm going to do after I get back." Trevor stirred the dough with a bit more force than necessary. "Actually it's none of your business."

Tyler shifted the coffeepot on the fire and clasped his hands together. "I promised her I wouldn't beat you, but you're testing my patience."

"Who did you promise? Nicky? It's none of her business either." There wasn't one nook or cranny in anyone's life that Nicky didn't poke her nose into. Good thing she was Trevor's sister or he might have to tell her to mind her own business too.

"You've been talking about this woman nonstop since we left Cheyenne. I'm just wondering if it will ever stop so I figured I'd ask what you planned on doing with her." Tyler used his neckerchief to pick up the pot and pour himself a cup of coffee.

Trevor put the frying pan on the fire to make the biscuits. "I have not been talking about her nonstop."

"That's a load of shit."

Tyler was not known for being subtle.

"It is not. It's true I've mentioned Adelaide, but nonstop? I don't think that's true." Trevor damn sure hoped it wasn't true. That would make him a lovesick idiot.

Was he a lovesick idiot? He'd sure as hell spent enough time thinking about her. Enough time to realize what he'd done was cowardly, and Tyler wouldn't let him even start making amends with a telegram.

Teaching him a lesson for sure.

A lesson that made him chomp at the bit like a green-broke horse.

ꕥ

Adelaide couldn't figure Brett out. On the one hand, he was quiet, yet when he did speak, there seemed to be an edge to his words. Sometimes a sharp edge. He didn't shout, or yell, or carry on like Trevor did, but she still felt as if he made certain he was heard. He stayed on at the Last Chance and helped Dustin repair the Silver Spittoon's fire damage. Always there in the shadows, Brett was like a guardian angel.

He clucked at her when she did too much, or when she tried something she shouldn't. With his eyes reflecting supreme disapproval, he'd assist her out of whatever pickle she'd gotten herself into. Yet he never chastised her, just sighed under his breath.

Brett appeared to be a thinker. A man who weighed every situation, even every word that came out of his mouth, before he made a decision. Adelaide was like Trevor in that she did things on the spur of the moment. In fact, Impulsive was likely Trevor's middle name. His big brother Brett's middle name was Cautious.

Almost two weeks after the telegram from Tyler, and over a month after being shot, Adelaide decided she was tired of coddling herself. She wanted to go for a ride, then have a beer and a big steak, followed by a game of poker. It sounded heavenly and there was no way in hell she'd let anyone stop her.

Although Brett decided to try.

He stood at the top of the stairs with his arms folded across his chest, wearing a blue shirt, black trousers and a frown.

"You're wearing a riding skirt."

Adelaide pulled on her gloves and stepped around him. "Your powers of observation are astounding, Brett."

He dogged her heels all the way down the stairs and into the street. "You can't go riding yet. It's only been a few weeks."

"It's been five and I'm sick of being inside. Look at this gorgeous summer weather. I need sunshine." Adelaide marched down to the livery where her quarter horse mare Blossom was stabled.

"I can't allow you to do this."

Adelaide stopped so suddenly, Brett ran into her back. Like being hit with a tree, she lost her breath and started falling forward, unable to prevent it. Brett somehow straddled her behind and threw out an arm to stop her from falling, and kept his left arm up in the air. Damned if it didn't look like he was riding a bronc. Not only that but he was pressed up so tightly against her backside, she swore she felt him harden.

"Let me up," Adelaide hissed.

Brett helped her to stand and cleared his throat about ten times in the process. She shooed his hands away and continued walking.

"You will never speak to me like that again, Brett Malloy. I am under no one else's control, particularly my lover's brother. What I do is my own business and no one else's. Is that clear?"

She couldn't see his face, but she knew just the same that he glared at her. Brett apparently didn't like outspoken women. Good thing he wasn't her lover.

"You could get hurt."

"I know that, but that's part of living life. Risks happen every time you open your eyes and greet the day." Adelaide reached the livery without another peep from Brett, but she knew he was back there, hovering.

"Good morning, Sam," Adelaide called as she stepped inside. The middle-aged man who ran the livery, Sam Johnson, walked over from oiling a saddle to greet her.

"Good morning, Miss Adelaide. You here to ride Blossom? She'll be glad of it, I'm thinking." He smiled his gap-toothed grin, which disappeared the moment he spotted Brett. "You own that big sorrel, right?"

Brett didn't say a word, but he must have nodded because Sam did the same.

"You planning on *escorting* Miss Adelaide?"

The emphasis Sam put on the word escorting wasn't lost on Brett. He strode forward and cupped Adelaide's elbow.

"I will make sure Adelaide is safe."

Safe.

Adelaide hadn't felt safe since Trevor left. Strange, she just realized that not only did she miss him, but she missed his presence. In his funny, cocky sort of way, Trevor made sure she was safe.

God, please keep him safe for me.

"It's okay, Sam. Brett is my shadow lately." Adelaide pulled away from his touch.

"You sure you're up to riding?" Sam took a blanket and headed into the barn.

"I'm fine." Adelaide pointedly looked at Brett and frowned.

Sam reappeared leading Blossom, and Adelaide's chest felt a hundred pounds lighter. Definitely the right decision to go riding. She petted Blossom's velvety nose, and she shook her dark mane, whickering as if to say "Where have you been?"

"I missed you too, girl."

Within minutes, Sam had her saddled and put the mounting block up for Adelaide. A twinge of pain echoed through her chest when she pulled herself into the saddle, but it was more muscle soreness from not doing anything rather than real pain.

"You be careful now," Sam warned as he led the mare out by the bit into the warm sunshine.

Brett sat waiting on his big sorrel, his careful blank expression on his face.

"I suppose you're going to follow me," Adelaide groused.

Brett gestured for her to precede him. She shook her head in puzzlement at Brett's odd ways, then spurred Blossom into a trot.

ഇര

By the time they reached Cheyenne, Trevor didn't feel anxious anymore. He felt plum loco, like a man who'd spent too long in the desert chewing on peyote. A week earlier, when they stopped in the town of Grayton for supplies, Tyler picked up a telegram from Dustin that indicated Adelaide was fine. When Trevor questioned him about it, Tyler grunted that he knew just how long it took to get from west Texas to Cheyenne and he'd told Dustin where to send a reply.

Trevor was frustrated with the answer, but knew he couldn't do a damn thing about it. However, the news about Adelaide was a welcome relief. The promise of seeing her alive and well was like dangling a damn carrot in front of a stupid mule. He plodded along trying desperately to grab it. Now it was within reach and apprehension raced through him.

The town didn't look any different from when he'd left, except for the new boards on the Silver Spittoon. Looked as if Dustin fixed it up after the fire.

What was different about it all was Trevor. He felt different, and not just because he'd gotten three bullet wounds in the past weeks. New scars inside and out. Trevor Malloy had finally decided to ask a woman to marry him.

"You might want to get a bath and a shave before you go see her." Tyler's voice broke through Trevor's thoughts.

"What?"

"You smell like the ass end of a horse, and I don't think you shaved in at least a week," Tyler noted.

"Oh, hell, I didn't even think about that. There's a bathing house a few blocks down."

It delayed his reunion with Adelaide, again, but in reality, he did smell. He didn't want her first reaction to be based on his stench. If he smelled clean, they could get closer. A lot closer.

"You're on your own now, Trevor," Tyler said as he turned toward the west. "I've got to meet Noah at the auction outside Laramie."

Trevor was actually sorry to see Tyler go. Sort of. He was a good man, even if he was a pain in the ass.

"Thank you for coming when I needed help. I, uh, really appreciate it." Trevor sighed. "I'm not good at this."

"Don't worry about it. I'll always come when you need help, that's what family is for."

It was the first time Tyler admitted Trevor was family. That made him grin from ear to ear.

"Nicky's wearing off on you."

"Don't remind me." Tyler tipped his hat back and leaned on the saddle horn. "Now take care of that girl of yours. Marry her. Good women don't come along every day, so don't waste your chance."

With that, Tyler adjusted his hat, nodded and rode off. Trevor shook his head and headed down the street to Nola's Bathing House. He really did smell like a horse's ass. He hoped he didn't act like one too.

ᏅᏣ

"You don't approve of Trevor," Adelaide mused as she and Brett watered the horses near a small stream just outside town.

His head snapped up and he wondered if she'd been reading his mind.

"I reckon it doesn't really matter what I think." The absolute truth in Brett's opinion. Trevor did whatever he felt like doing, no matter what Brett said.

Sometimes Brett wondered if he'd been adopted, but he looked too much like his brothers for that to be true. If only he were a bit more fun-loving like Trevor, or funny like Jack, or even personable like Ethan. No, he had to be the quiet one. The brother who spent so much time keeping his mouth shut folks thought he was either touched in the head or unsociable.

Like it was a crime to keep your thoughts to yourself. If he didn't, Adelaide would discover that he really wanted her for himself. That he'd lain awake nearly every night for weeks wanting to kiss her, to see if she felt as good as he imagined.

But dammit all, she was his brother's woman. Spoken for, plain and simple. If Trevor threw her away, Brett would kick his ass, then ask Adelaide to marry him. At thirty-three, Brett didn't have a whole lot of time before he needed to get busy making babies and finding a wife.

The spicy little redhead in front of him would do nicely, unfortunately, she wasn't available.

"Of course it matters," Adelaide said as she started to walk along the bank of the stream.

It took Brett a moment or two to figure out what she was talking about.

"Trevor does whatever he wants to do, no matter what anyone else says or thinks, so no, it doesn't matter." Brett knew he sounded a bit harsh, but hell, he just couldn't sugarcoat anything.

Adelaide scowled at him. "You don't think your opinion matters to your brother?"

"No, that's not what I meant. It's like this." Brett stepped closer to Adelaide, breathing in the soft, sweet scent of woman that immediately made him hungry for more. "Trevor hears whatever anyone says, he just never listens to it."

Brett moved away before he did something stupid like try to kiss her.

"Ah, I see what you mean. That's probably very true. I think we're alike in that respect. I hear, but I don't always listen either."

Brett snorted.

"Yes?" The haughty tone of Adelaide's voice made Brett snort again.

"You never listen and don't try to shovel any more shit because it's already knee deep."

Adelaide burst out laughing, a belly-deep laugh that made her whole face light up and her eyes sparkle. Brett felt a smile playing around his lips as her mirth dove under his skin and tickled his sleeping funny bone.

"Oh...my...God!" Adelaide pointed at him and held her stomach with one arm. "I saw a smile."

By sheer force of will Brett held back the grin that threatened. Adelaide was charming, beautiful and sexy enough to actually give him wet dreams at his age.

Dammit, if Trevor didn't get home in the next two days, then to hell with brotherly courtesy.

Brett wanted Adelaide.

Chapter Seventeen

Trevor emerged from the bathing house a changed man, literally. After a long soak in which he nearly scrubbed himself raw, he paid for a hot shave and a splash of cologne. He pulled out semi-clean clothes from his saddlebags to put the finishing touches on his dapper appearance. They were a bit wrinkled, but didn't smell bad. Trevor glanced down and decided he looked and smelled good.

Time to go courting his lady.

His lady. His *woman*. He'd never thought that phrase would ever ring true. Trevor had spent his life having fun, having sex, and living life for the moment. Now thoughts crowded his brain about marriage, children and the rest of his life.

Damn, it was for the rest of his life. Was he ready for that? Seeing his brothers and sister enjoying married life gave him hope that he would find the same joy they had. The thought of one woman for the next fifty years actually sent a shiver down his spine and he broke out in a cold sweat.

One woman. Forever.

Trevor stopped his juvenile panic from spreading. He was knee deep in love with Adelaide. No, not knee deep. He was in it up to his eyeballs. Not a day had gone by in the last few weeks that he hadn't missed her, and not just in the bedroom. He missed her sass, her laugh, her touch, her wit. Jesus, he missed everything about her.

Oh yeah, one woman. Forever and ever. Trevor was well and truly caught in Cupid's net.

That decision made, Trevor stepped off the sidewalk to walk across the street. He spotted Brett and Adelaide riding toward the livery together. Adelaide was laughing and reached over to touch Brett's shoulder.

Holy shit.

Brett smiled.

Holy shit again.

Brett *never* smiled. That only meant one thing. He wanted Adelaide for himself. Trevor broke into a run, leaving his horse and saddlebags behind. No fucking way he'd lose the woman he loved to his brother. Not when he'd just found her.

When Adelaide tried to dismount, Brett stood beneath her with his arms up. Apparently when he wanted to, Brett could be a gentleman. She leaned into his hands and he plucked her off the horse like she weighed nothing, which was far from the truth.

As her feet touched the ground, Brett's hands lingered longer than necessary. She looked up into his eyes and wasn't surprised to see lust plainly written there. He'd been exuding arousal for a while; she'd just chosen to ignore it.

Now she'd have to tell him to leave.

"Brett, I—"

"Adelaide!"

Trevor's shout made her nearly jump a foot. Her eyes pricked with tears and she wondered if she imagined him calling her. Brett dropped his hands and stepped away. Adelaide turned to see Trevor coming toward them at a dead run.

Alive! Not only was he alive, but healthy too or he wouldn't be running down the street like a maniac. Her heart beat a staccato rhythm at the sheer joy she felt at seeing him. Even her fingers tingled and her smile felt as wide as the Mississippi River. It had been so long—too long. Thank God he'd come back.

"Trevor!" Adelaide ran toward him, heedless of the pinch of pain in her chest at the effort.

When she reached him, he opened his arms and she threw herself at him. He stumbled backwards a step or two, then wrapped himself around her and held on so tightly she could barely get a breath. A few tears leaked out of her eyes as she breathed in his scent, his essence. Her body sighed with joy to have him in her arms again.

"God, I missed you." His voice sounded husky and a bit shaky.

"Me, too, cowboy," she whispered against his neck.

Trevor cupped her face and kissed her hard, almost bruisingly. She took it and served back a fierceness that had him opening his mouth against hers. Tongues danced and slid as remembered passions flared between them.

"Welcome back, Trevor," Brett said from behind her.

Trevor lifted his head and the look in his eyes changed from passion to fury in a blink. He kissed her one last time, then set her to the side.

"You crossed the line, brother." Trevor's voice rang with anger. "I saw you. I saw what you were doing. You never fucking smile and there you were looking to make Adelaide yours, weren't you?"

"What? Trevor, are you loco?" Adelaide tried to insert herself between them, but Trevor gently stopped her.

"This is between me and him, honey." He turned his attention back to Brett. "She's mine."

Brett's mouth pinched into a white line. "You left her. In fact, you left her in my hands without even sending a telegram for weeks."

Trevor pushed at Brett's shoulder. "That doesn't mean you can have her. Your hands were never meant to actually touch her, Brett. She's *mine*," he repeated.

Adelaide felt like she'd stepped into a fight between two cavemen and she was the prize. No way she'd allow that to happen. She put a hand flat on each of their chests, their thundering hearts beating against her palms. "There won't be a fight here today, boys."

"Oh yes there will," Trevor said right before he swung at Brett.

Brett ducked and threw a right punch into Trevor's stomach. And that started a knock-down, drag-out fight in the middle of the Cheyenne street. Adelaide, while grateful they were outside, couldn't help but wonder what possessed men to fight. It was never about words with them; it was always about force.

Within moments, Dustin stood at her side, watching the brothers roll around in the dust punching each other. She swore she even saw some hair pulling and biting. It seemed that this fight had been a long time coming.

"How long they been at it?" Dustin asked.

"Just a few minutes. I expect once they get it out of their systems, they'll stop."

"Let's hope it's before one kills the other."

Dustin's prediction forced Adelaide into ending the fight before something deadly really did happen. She marched over to the horse trough, grabbed a bucket beside it, and scooped up some water. When she got back to the Malloys, they were still grunting and punching each other. Bloody noses, lips and a black eye or two were already visible.

"Stop fighting this instant or I'll stop you," Adelaide warned.

Apparently Malloys didn't like to listen when they were punching each other, because they ignored her. Adelaide glanced at Dustin who shrugged and gestured to the bucket. With the thought that she hoped Trevor would forgive her, she upended the water on them with a mighty splash.

The end result seemed to be worth the dousing. They immediately broke apart and rolled away, sputtering and shaking like the dogs they'd been behaving like.

"That's better. Now there will be no more fighting." Adelaide handed the bucket to Dustin who appeared as though he wanted to bust out laughing.

Trevor regarded her with an accusing, hurt gaze. "Why did you do that?"

She helped him to his feet and surveyed the damage. Torn, dirty clothes, and plenty of wounds and blood to clean up. Brett stood and tried to dust off his pants, without looking at either of them.

"Let's go inside and get you two fixed up. I'm sure Marybeth will be happy to see you like this." Adelaide took Trevor's arm and walked toward the saloon. When she glanced behind her, Brett wasn't there. "Where's Brett?"

Trevor snorted. "I don't give a shit. He can go to hell for all I care."

"Not nice, Malloy. He's your brother."

"He tried to take you from me." Now Trevor sounded like a little boy.

"No, he didn't. He protected me, fussed over me and nagged me, but he never tried to take me.

"I saw what I saw," Trevor said petulantly.

Adelaide shook her head. "Well, I hope he comes back to the saloon when he settles down."

Trevor didn't respond to her hope. They walked back to The Last Chance together, Adelaide's joy overshadowed by the brothers' fight.

ཀྱ

"Well, I'm certainly not surprised," Marybeth clucked as she dipped the rag into the basin of water on the table in the kitchen. "Your pretty face isn't so pretty right now."

Trevor hissed when she touched the cloth to a cut above his right eye. "Ow."

"Baby. Just sit still."

Trevor scowled and sat still for Marybeth's not-so-subtle ministrations.

"You look awful," Marybeth continued.

Adelaide sat at the table with her chin resting on her fist, watching Marybeth work.

"I was all gussied up and clean before I saw Adelaide. I even smelled good." Trevor sighed.

"You'll need another bath, and clean clothes. I think you left some here." Marybeth finished cleaning all the wounds and frowned at his shirt and trousers. "Those will need to be sewed. Foolish men."

"You know I love you, Marybeth, but if you don't stop I'm going to have to get mad." Trevor wasn't in the mood to verbally spar with her.

"Thank you, Marybeth," Adelaide finally spoke, forestalling a shouting match between Trevor and his surly nurse.

With a sniff and a grumbled curse, Marybeth stomped out of the kitchen, wearing an annoyed expression. Adelaide rose and circled round the table to stand beside Trevor. Her fingers sifted through his dusty hair, the brown waves full of dirt and twigs.

"You really are dirty, you know." She leaned against him, her body heat seeping into his.

Her scent filled his nose, awakening his sleeping arousal with a snarl. He wrapped his arms around her waist and pressed his face into her belly. The unbelievable sensation of holding her in his arms was enough to make him close his eyes against tears. How he missed her, loved her, needed her.

"Red, I...I'm sorry for leaving." He reached up to kiss the spot where she'd been shot. "God, I'm so sorry," Trevor choked out.

Adelaide caressed his cheek and he kissed her palm.

"I love you, Trevor Malloy."

At first he thought he'd heard her wrong. "What?"

"You heard me, pretty boy. I love you." She pulled him to a standing position, although she probably had no idea his legs were shaking so hard he could barely hold himself up.

Trevor swallowed the enormous lump in his throat and looked down into Adelaide's beautiful eyes. Into the eyes that held his future, his heart and his soul.

"I-I love you too, honey."

With that his mouth captured hers in a kiss he felt all the way to his toes. Finally, *finally.*

As their kiss turned into two, then three, then countless kisses, Trevor's staff lengthened and hardened to painful proportions. He had to have her. It had been too long.

He didn't have to say anything, she broke the kiss and waggled her eyebrows. "Let's go upstairs, cowboy."

Adelaide locked the door behind them, her heart beating madly and her breathing already choppy. As if a fever had taken hold of her, she was overcome with need, with lust for Trevor. She yanked off his filthy clothes, leaving what was left on the floor between them. In seconds, her riding skirt and blouse followed his garments. As she stood in her chemise and bloomers, Trevor's gaze traveled over her half-dressed body.

"My God, you're perfect." The reverence in his voice could not be faked. That was the gift of love.

"I'm glad you're blind, Trevor," she joked in a shaky voice.

He kneeled in front of her and kissed her belly. "You smell so good." He nipped at the tender skin around her rib cage and a shiver danced up her skin, leaving goose bumps in its wake. Soon his hands pushed her chemise slowly up, kissing and licking the exposed skin, skirting her nipples until he stood and pulled it completely off.

He gently kissed her pink scar, as if apologizing. Trevor cupped her breasts and ran his thumbs over the hardened nipples. A sharp throb of desire pulsed through her, landing between her legs where her pussy grew plump with arousal. Back on his knees, he licked her nipple like a kitten while he started tugging down her bloomers.

He nibbled, then bit her, eliciting a gasp of pleasure.

"Do that again," Adelaide commanded.

Trevor complied, biting a bit harder. Her bloomers flew off, and his hand found her hot core, ready for him. Two fingers teased and rubbed her clit while another dipped into her. Adelaide moved with him, sliding on his nimble digits, reaching for the pleasure she knew he could give her.

His other hand skimmed around and teased her other hole, the one that had never been visited before Trevor. While a finger slid inside her, he bit and sucked her nipple, and pinched her hot button. The combination of the three sent Adelaide over the precipice of ecstasy. She flew on wings of rapture as his mouth and hands carried her on the wind.

After the waves subsided, Adelaide felt languid yet still aroused. She needed more. She needed Trevor. He stood and scooped her up in his arms, heading for the bed. Adelaide had never had a man do that before and she figured she wouldn't protest. It felt too much like a fairy tale.

Trevor laid her down and immediately covered her body with his. His weight pushed down on her chest too hard and she hissed in pain. He rolled onto his back, and pulled her so she straddled him. Tracing the scar with his fingers, he apologized with his eyes.

"It's okay, darling. I'd do it again in an instant if it meant I could save your life."

"Adelaide," he whispered, that one word holding a lifetime of promise and a heart full of love.

Adelaide leaned down and ran her tongue along the seam of his lips. Licking his mouth while his breath mixed with hers. When she finally kissed him, her whole body sighed with relief. Fused as one, she kissed him with everything she felt, an outpouring of what Trevor meant to her.

He kissed her back, with as much love as she gave him. Her breasts brushed against his chest, the hairs lightly tickling her nipples. Trevor's hands traced her spine, his fingertips caressing the dips and curves in her back. When he reached her ass, he pulled her down so her legs spread wider, right onto his erection.

Hot, sizzling, pulsing heat between them, Adelaide welcomed him into her body. She angled herself just right and he slid into her like a key in a well-oiled lock.

Perfect.

"Ride me," he said against her lips.

Adelaide needed no encouragement. She moved up and down at an even pace, savoring the fullness, the pleasure, the absolute rightness of making love to Trevor. Their breaths came in short gasps, their skin heated and rubbed together. She expected their first reunion to be more of a fierce mating. Instead, it was slow, sweet loving that solidified their love.

She sat up, pushing him deeper inside her so she couldn't tell where he ended and she began, sending a spear of ecstasy through her. The walls of her pussy clenched around him.

"Yes, baby, yes," he crooned, pinching her nipples.

Adelaide gazed into his eyes as she reached for her peak. Closer, closer, nearly there. One of his hands rubbed her clit and she snapped. Her body convulsed around him as waves of pleasure crashed through her over and over. Trevor held onto her hips as he came, shouting her name and pouring the seed of life deep within her body.

Winded and spent, Adelaide lay down on his chest. Perspiration made her slippery, and she chuckled when she slid sideways. He wrapped his arms around her and kissed her neck.

"I love you, Red."

She smiled at the nickname that she used to hate, but now loved since the man who used it owned her heart.

"Love you too, Trevor."

ꙮ

Brett stood outside the Last Chance Saloon in the cover of darkness, embracing the solitude he'd found. He'd had more than a few whiskeys with Dustin. The big bartender seemed to understand that Brett needed silence, so Dustin didn't offer the inane conversation most folks had.

A pleasant buzz slipped through his body after the fourth whiskey. Without food, the amber liquid shot straight to his head. Good thing Trevor hadn't appeared again, and especially Adelaide. He'd have done or said something really stupid.

Brett wasn't a young boy, nor was he stupid. Adelaide had chosen Trevor, which left Brett with no one to warm his bed or his life. It was as cold as it ever was.

He'd been away from home for more than a month, no doubt there was plenty of work to be done. He wouldn't find a woman on the Malloy ranch who wasn't married or related to him.

Brett took a deep breath and pushed away from the wall on unsteady feet. Time to go home.

Chapter Eighteen

After half a day in bed rediscovering each other's bodies, Trevor and Adelaide emerged in the afternoon with wide grins and twinges of sore muscles. They'd also spent the time talking, about everything and everybody. Adelaide realized Trevor would make peace in time with Brett so she didn't push the issue.

When they entered the kitchen, Marybeth was already washing dishes. After glancing at them holding hands, she harrumphed and turned her back to them.

"You could help out, you know." She raised an eyebrow at Trevor. "Or are your hands too busy with Adelaide?"

"We have a proposition for you, Marybeth." Trevor poured two cups of coffee from the pot on the stove and handed one to a smiling Adelaide.

"What kind of proposition?" Suspicion laced the older woman's tone.

Trevor sat at the table and sipped the hot brew. "Not that kind."

Adelaide chuckled. "No, not that kind. I want to give you the Silver Spittoon to turn into a restaurant."

Marybeth's face drained of color and she dropped like a rock into a chair. Her mouth opened and closed several times before she spoke. "What?"

"I don't need two saloons, especially one across from the other. So I thought a restaurant would be a better choice. You are an amazing cook, and well, it would give you more privacy," Adelaide explained.

"Why would you do this? It's your property fair and square." Marybeth almost sounded touched.

"Because you're my family and I want to." Adelaide leaned over and embraced her quickly. "There is one condition though."

Dustin slammed into the kitchen with a scowl. "Okay, here I am. What the hell is going on?"

"Perfect timing, big man." Trevor gestured to the chair across from Marybeth.

Although his expression indicated he didn't want to, Dustin sat down anyway with a scowl. "Get to it, pretty boy."

"We've asked Marybeth to open a restaurant where the Silver Spittoon is, actually own the building too. On one condition," Adelaide explained, a grin playing around her mouth.

"A restaurant? Well, she can cook." Dustin's compliments needed work.

"The condition? What is it?" Marybeth interjected.

"That you take on a partner. A permanent partner."

It took Dustin and Marybeth a few beats to puzzle out what Adelaide meant.

"You want me to marry her?" Dustin shouted.

"Marry that big galoot?" Marybeth pushed back from the table.

Adelaide held up her hands and they both stopped grousing. "It's been obvious to me for years that you two love each other. Stop denying it and do something about it."

"Life's too short to let your pride stand in your way," Trevor added. "I wasted too much time realizing that Adelaide was my life."

Marybeth looked at Dustin with a question in her brown eyes. He opened his mouth, then closed it. With a glare leveled at Adelaide, then at Trevor, Dustin stood.

Adelaide's heart nearly wept at the hurt she saw in Marybeth's eyes.

"I reckon we might as well do what they ask." He held out his hand to Marybeth.

No one could have convinced Adelaide she would ever see Marybeth cry, but damned if a tear didn't escape from her left eye.

"Well, okay."

Not the most romantic of proposals, especially since Dustin held out his hand for Marybeth to shake on it, but it would do.

Adelaide grinned at Trevor who winked back.

After they worked out the details, Dustin and Marybeth headed off to their new restaurant. There was definitely hope for them after Adelaide noticed Dustin held the door for her.

Trevor stood behind Adelaide and slid his arms around her waist. He nuzzled her ear and kissed the lobe.

"Feel like playing poker, Red?" he whispered.

Adelaide laughed and leaned back into Trevor. "Let's go, cowboy."

ഇന്ദ

Writing to his parents to explain what happened was a helluva lot harder than Trevor expected. What could he say? Sorry to have been such an ass and a selfish shit?

He sat there for two hours in Adelaide's office on Sunday night while she dealt poker in the saloon. After wracking his brains to try to come up with something, he simply scrunched up the paper, threw it across the room and smacked his head on the desk.

Cool, soft hands touched his neck.

"Give up already?" Adelaide asked.

Trevor sat up and looked at her with a sigh. "I don't know what to say."

She slid onto his lap and kissed his cheek. "Start with 'I'm sorry' and then 'Please come to Cheyenne'."

Was it that simple? Is that all he needed to do? Apologize and invite them?

"Do you think it will work?"

She bit his earlobe. "Of course it will work. Everybody loves you, Trevor."

So early Monday morning, Trevor sent a telegram to his parents then went back to the saloon and threw back a whiskey. The good stuff, not the rotgut Dustin drank. Thank God the big man was spending most of his time over at the restaurant. Trevor filled in as bartender until they could find someone reliable.

Marybeth had hired a new kitchen boy for the restaurant—McGee's son Alex. The boy turned out to be a hard worker who bonded with the older woman immediately.

A week after Trevor sent the telegram, they were having Sunday morning breakfast with Marybeth and Dustin at the restaurant when a wagon pulled up in front of the Last Chance. Adelaide noticed it first.

"Who are all those people?"

Trevor jumped to his feet, eggs and toast forgotten, and saw the crowd. "My family."

His stomach immediately tied itself into a knot. This was what he'd been dreading, the confrontation. He'd left home on lousy terms and basically abandoned his family. Adelaide slipped her hand into his and smiled.

"Can I meet them?"

He squeezed her hand and they walked out together into the street. The first thing he noticed was that Jack and Ray were arguing, as usual. Ethan stood to the side with his hands on his hips, shaking his head. His father was helping his mother down from the wagon. Noah sat on the bench, reins in hand. He was the first to notice Trevor and Adelaide and waved.

The butterflies in Trevor's stomach had nothing on the sick feeling that crept up his throat. He crossed the street to greet his family.

"Trevor!" His mother saw him and broke into a wide grin. "Oh, hurry up, John."

His father grumbled under his breath and finally set her on her feet. "There, you happy now?"

She immediately met them and before they could step onto the sidewalk, grabbed Trevor into a back-cracking hug. Trevor felt the weight of his guilt lift at her enthusiastic greeting.

"*Ma petit.* It is so good to see you." Her accent grew thicker when she was emotional. "And this is your lady." She kissed Adelaide on both cheeks. "Welcome to the family, Adelaide."

The surprise on Adelaide's face would have made him laugh if he wasn't dreading his father's greeting. He needn't have worried though.

John Malloy simply hugged his son and said, "Good to see you well, boy."

He greeted Adelaide very politely, and even kissed her hand. Adelaide reacted by actually blushing. Trevor couldn't help but laugh at that, until she punched his arm.

"Sorry everyone couldn't come," Jack said as he approached them. The youngest of the Malloy siblings, he shared the blue eyes of Brett, and the jovial nature of the clown in the family. He always had a smile at the ready. "Nicky and Tyler just got some new colts in that they're training. Bonita, Becky and Lily had to stay home with the kids. No use sharing the he—I mean scaring your lady right off."

He stepped up to Adelaide and winked. "Nice to finally meet the woman who lassoed this cowboy."

Adelaide raised one eyebrow. "I see Trevor didn't get all the charm."

Jack grinned and hugged her quickly. "You'll do just fine I think."

Ethan's grin and polite greeting followed. It was hard to believe Ethan was the same brother who had pounded him in a whorehouse three months earlier.

His oldest brother Ray finally stepped toward them, a frown creasing his brow. Not that it was unusual, Ray frowned a lot. Now that he'd found his wife, Lily, it wasn't a constant frown, but it still appeared pretty regularly.

His gaze assessed both of them, flickering back and forth until he apparently found what he was looking for. He stuck out his hand and Trevor shook it, hoping a punch wouldn't follow since the last time they'd seen each other he'd laid out Ray on the floor of their parents' house.

"Glad to see you're alive, little brother. About time you found your own woman." He nodded and tipped his hat to Adelaide. "Ma'am."

Noah hopped down and said hello, then the Malloy clan trooped noisily into the Last Chance Saloon.

"Feel better?" Adelaide wrapped her arm around his waist and walked slowly toward the building.

"Yep, sure do. Thanks for making me do this."

She waved her hand in dismissal. "I didn't make you do it. You needed to do it."

Adelaide was right. The only shadow that still crept around the corner was Brett. Trevor was certain that when the time was right, he'd come back and make peace.

For now, he'd acknowledge the rest of his family's acceptance and welcome to Adelaide. He took a deep cleansing breath and stared at the sign above the saloon.

"You know, I think we ought to change the name to the Five Thousand Marker. What do you think?"

Adelaide laughed and hugged him. "Sounds like a great idea, pretty boy."

Trevor and Adelaide walked into the saloon to start the rest of their lives. Together.

About the Author

You can't say cowboys without thinking of Beth Williamson. She likes 'em hard, tall and packing. Read her work and discover for yourself how hot and dangerous a cowboy can be.

Beth lives in North Carolina, with her husband and two sons. Born and raised in New York, she holds a B.F.A. in writing from New York University. She spends her days as a technical writer, and her nights immersed in writing hot romances for her readers.

To learn more about Beth Williamson, please visit www.bethwilliamson.com. Send an email to Beth at mailto:beth@bethwilliamson.com, join her Yahoo! Group, http://groups.yahoo.com/group/cowboylovers, or sign up for Beth's monthly newsletter, Sexy Spurs, http://www.crocodesigns.com/cgi-bin/dada/mail.cgi/list/spurs/

Look for these titles

Now Available

The Bounty
The Prize
The Reward
The Treasure

Coming Soon:

The Tribute
The Legacy
Devils on Horseback: Nate

What happens when a bounty hunter finds his prey only to discover she's his mate?

The Bounty

© 2006 Beth Williamson

Book 1 of the Malloy family series.

Nicky Malloy is on the run—from guilt, fear, and a murder charge. After three years, the notorious bounty hunter Tyler Calhoun catches up with the elusive lady outlaw. The intensity of their dislike for each other is only matched by the growing passion they cannot seem to control.

A loner by nature, a cold hard hunter by choice, Tyler fights his feelings for his prisoner the only way he knows how—by denying them. He's not prepared for how deeply his feelings will run, or how hard it will be to hold her life in his hands.

Pursued by two hapless cowboys bent on taking Nicky in themselves, Nicky and Tyler are forced to turn to each other for aid, trust, and comfort as their journey progresses on its rocky road. Caught in a web of lies and murder, they hold on to each other as they travel to Wyoming to confront the man that brought them together. Tyler has to decide if his love for her is worth more than the bounty he was sent to find.

This book has been previously published, but substantially revised and reedited.

Warning, this title contains the following: explicit sex, graphic language, some violence.

Available now in ebook and print from Samhain Publishing.

Enjoy the following excerpt...

Over the next several days, Nicky took it upon herself to study Tyler Calhoun, to gather all the information she could about the tight-lipped bounty hunter. Something she could use to escape, a weakness, anything. Trying to keep her plans unknown, she studied him when she thought he wasn't looking. As they rode side by side across the plains each day, he never seemed to be interested in her at all, which gave her the opportunity to complete her surreptitious study.

She decided that he truly was as extremely handsome as she had originally thought. He had a broad chest and shoulders, narrow waist and hips, and thick black hair which all fit together in one nice package. His jaw was set in a hard line, his chin was covered with light stubble only hours after he shaved, his nose was straight and fine, his thick mustache rode a pair of lips that were just the right size for kissing.

She had to stop thinking about kissing him. It was a one time occurrence—never to repeat itself. If she kept telling herself that, she might believe it.

It was his eyes that truly haunted her. She'd never seen eyes quite that shade of blue before. They suddenly flicked over to hers. He had caught her looking at him. Chagrined by her actions as well as her pitiful, susceptible heart, she affixed him with an innocent look.

"You've been staring at me for two days. Something you need, Nicole?"

She didn't trust that soft tone for anything.

"Yes." She scrambled for a reason. "Since this is going to be a long journey, I thought we could at least talk. The silence is making me jumpy."

He shook his head, then turned his gaze forward again. Nicky squeezed her lips together in determination. Now he'd pissed her off by dismissing her. She would make him talk.

"How long have you been a bounty hunter?"

The silence was only broken by the sound of the horses' hooves clopping on the hard-packed dirt and the jangle of the chain that bound them together.

"Have you caught many men?"

Still nothing. He obviously underestimated a woman that grew up with six older brothers. She could be a pest's pest when she wanted to. Time to get dirty.

"Was Hermano the first time you'd been captured? How embarrassing."

Clip-clop went the horses' hooves.

"Where are you from? Texas? Sounds like it. You went all the way from Texas to Wyoming for this job? Owen must have waved a lot of money under your nose."

His hands tightened on the reins, and she smiled at his growing impatience.

"Wife? Children? Friends? Enemies? Favorite things to do?"

Tyler finally turned his head toward her. His eyes glittered like chips of blue ice, cold and hard.

"You're worth six thousand dollars to me...alive, anyway. That's all you need to know. What makes you ask all these questions about me?" His tone certainly did not match the look on his face.

Her heart dropped along with her stomach. They were dragging behind the horse now.

Six thousand dollars. That's a damned fortune. Who in their right mind would turn that down to capture an outlaw?

“Ah, well, ah...y-you seem to know, um, to know everything there is to know about me...” she stammered.

His gaze raked up and down her body. Those ice blue eyes found hers. His expression hadn’t changed. “No, not everything,” he said as he turned away from her again.

“You know more than most men,” she retorted.

His head snapped back to hers. The coldness had intensified in his eyes. Thankfully, the sun burst through the clouds at that moment and the brim of his hat shaded most of his face.

“Have you known many men? Like Nate maybe? I couldn’t find you in any whorehouse, but maybe that means you had your own business going. You’re a nice piece of calico—it could happen.”

Nice piece of calico?

Now she was getting angry. She was no whore, dammit. And one kiss didn’t change that fact. She yanked on the chain that bound her to his saddle. Tyler grabbed the chain tightly with one hand.

“What I have or have not done with men is none of your damned business, Calhoun. Why are you being so all-fired nasty to me?”

“I could ask you the same question.”

“All I wanted to do was pass the time. You wouldn’t talk so...I made you talk. I win.”

He snorted. “Bullshit, Malloy. Now shut up and keep riding.”

His voice was firm as he kneed his horse to a faster pace.

“I still win. Can we stop for dinner?”

He didn’t answer her.

"I will throw myself from my horse and drag you down with me," she said sweetly but with a touch of ice. "If you don't stop and let me rest."

Calhoun turned to look at her. She saw a flash of something—irritation?—cross his features, then he was his cool self again.

"As long as you'll stop your blathering, magpie," he said through his clenched teeth.

So, too much talking bothered him? She wasn't normally a chatterbox, but being talkative could be an easy weapon to wield against her captor. Oh, joy! She mentally rubbed her hands together at her newly found bit of information.

"Thank you, Calhoun," she cooed with a bright smile.

Tyler snorted at her thanks. He stopped the horses at a small pond, and dismounted in one fluid motion. He unlocked the shackles from the saddle horn and reached his arms up to lift her down.

Nicky's arm bumped the brim of her hat, knocking it off and letting her curls loose like a small explosion of hair. They tumbled down, brushing Tyler's face.

Nicky caught her breath at the desire she saw flame in Tyler's eyes. His hands felt like branding irons on her sides. Ever so slowly, her feet touched the ground. Her breathing quickened as they stood between the horses, his hands still on her waist.

Kiss me.

It seemed like a moment frozen in time, as if they existed outside here and now. Nicky licked her lips as she searched Tyler's eyes. For what, she didn't know. She could smell his scent exuding from him like a beckoning knell. She breathed deeply, inhaling Tyler into her body. She raised her hand to his face. When her fingertips made contact with his cheek, he didn't jerk away. He closed his eyes. Nicky would swear she felt him shudder.

She didn't dare take a breath. The moment was as fragile as a butterfly's wing.

Kiss me.

In answer to her silent plea, Tyler's eyes opened and he pulled her to him hard as his mouth descended on her parted lips. His body was long and muscled but curved into hers like a key in a lock. Nicky expected his lips to be as hard as the rest of him, but they were soft and demanding. His mustache tickled her cheeks, sending delightful shivers down her back. His tongue was tracing the outline of her lips.

So sweet, so sensual. God, it was like heaven.

Her heart was hammering against her ribcage so loudly she was sure Tyler must hear it. Uttering a small moan, she opened her mouth to his slick tongue and pressed herself against him fully, her hands probing his muscled chest. This is what she wanted, what she craved, what she *needed.*

Tyler released a primitive, animal-like noise deep in his throat as his hands roamed up and down her back. One hand settled on her behind, squeezing gently. The other anchored itself in her hair. His tongue delved into the dark recesses of her mouth where no man had ever been.

Nicky's head was spinning as she kissed him with every fiber of her being. Every nerve ending jangled, every inch of skin sang. Her breasts felt constrained in her chambray shirt. Her jeans felt too tight as an incredible ache between her legs intensified with the kiss. The rawness of her reaction was frightening.

Nicky clung to Tyler for dear life as a near maelstrom swirled inside her. *Never,* never had she felt anything like this for a man.